T0266198

—Other math books by Theoni Pappas—

The Joy of Mathematics
More Joy of Mathematics
The Mathematics Calendar
Magic of Mathematics
Mathematical Scandals
The Music of Reason
Math Talk
Greek Cooking For Everyone
Math-A-Day
Mathematical Footprints
Math Stuff
Math Talk
Do the math!
Puzzles from Penrose
Number and other math ideas come alive
Mathematical Journeys

Fractals, Googols & Other Mathematical Tales
Math for Kids & Other People Too!
The Adventures of Penrose
The Further Adventures of Penrose
More Adventures from Penrose

The Further ADVENTURES of Penrose the mathematical cat

by theoni pappas

WIDE WORLD PUBLISHING/TETRA

Wide World Publishing
P.O. Box 476
San Carlos, CA 94070
websites:
http://wideworldpublishing.com

7th Printing June 2021

Library of Congress Cataloging-in-Publication Data

Pappas, Theoni
The further adventures of Penrose : The mathematical cat / by Theoni
Pappas .

p.   cm.

Summary : Penrose is back, and ready to usher young readers along as he encounters more amazing mathematical ideas in a sequence of adventure tales. At once demystifying and challenging, the book gives readers visuals to consider and things to do as they - along with Penrose - discover mathematical "rep-tiles"; meet x, the mathematical actor; find out when one and one do not equal two; help Sorry Snowflake find its symmetry; cross pi's path; learn that mathematical donuts are not for dunking; and more. Plus, Penrose tantalizes, teases, and perplexes with his puzzles and games around every corner. Like Pappas's other acclaimed mathematics books for children, these amusing and informative stories are designed to stimulate the imagination and motivate young minds to think about, grasp, and even marvel over concepts they might otherwise shy away from. A good bet for Pappas fans, Penrose fans, math buffs, teachers, students, and parents.

ISBN: 1884550320 (pbk.)
        9781884550324 (pbk.)
1. Mathematics -- Study and teaching (Elementary)
[1 . Mathematics.] I . Title .

                                    2012392932
                                    CIP
                                    AC

iv

For Lucy, Snowpea, Noah
and Elvira
all really cool cats

TABLE OF CONTENTS

Preface

As I mentioned in **The Adventures of Penrose,** Penrose's interest in mathematics started when he was just a kitten. He always got into my papers, played with my puzzles, and at times he appeared to be turning pages in my various mathematics books. I thought he might outgrow his playfulness and interest in mathematics, but no, now as a cat he is even more curious about math. Even a closed office door doesn't stop him from finding a way to enter. At first I thought he was only interested in getting my attention, but he has a mathematical curiosity that won't stop as you will discover from his latest adventures. Penrose continues to spark my imagination. Perhaps he will do the same for you.

—Theoni Pappas

Every chapter is self-contained. You can open the book at random and discover and enjoy a mathematical idea, game, or puzzle which is independent of any of the others.

Penrose watches a spider spin math

"Hey, furball. What are you staring at?" The orb spider yelled at Penrose.

The spider smiled and in a gentle voice said, "Thank you."

"You know it actually outlines an equiangular spiral," Penrose continued.

"An equiang-what?" the spider asked.

"An e - qui - an - gu - lar spiral." Penrose slowly enunciated the word. "One of the beautiful shapes of mathematics."

Hey! furball. What are you staring at?

Your web.

"Your web," Penrose replied, feeling a bit indignant at being called furball.

"What's wrong with my web?" the spider asked.

"Nothing," Penrose answered. "It's pretty amazing."

"I don't know anything about mathematics. I just do what comes naturally," the spider responded. "Why is it called equiangular?"

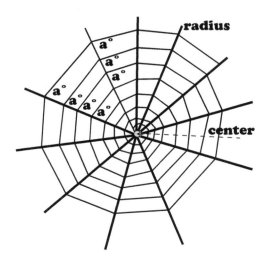

"Look how each line segment from the spiral's center makes the same angle with the connecting segments of your web all the way around the web," Penrose explained pointing with his paw. "You know what else is wonderful about equiangular spirals?"

"What?" asked the spider.

"No matter how small or how large the spiral is made, it retains the same shape throughout. Actually an equiangular spiral can grow inward or outward forever," Penrose said.

"In that case, maybe I'll make a huge web," the spider said, "but I guess I'd

better be careful of what I might trap. Come to think of it, I've seen that spiral elsewhere," the spider added.

"Really? Where?" Penrose asked.

Where?

"On many shells and on the head of a little boy I landed on one day. His hair was growing in that spiral shape," the spider answered.

"I'm not surprised. Nature uses it and other spirals in designing many of its things. It's an amazing curve," Penrose said.

"Why do you call it amazing?" the spider asked.

"Because it also appears in mathe- matical objects," Penrose replied. "Look at how it is hidden in this group of golden rectangles. Watch it appear as I draw arcs in each square inside the rectangle."

"There's an equiangular spiral!" the spider shouted. "That's impressive."

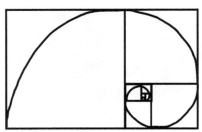

"One of my favorite ways it appears in math is from an isosceles right triangle," Penrose said as he drew one.

"I don't believe it," the spider replied skeptically.

Penrose didn't lose a beat, and continued to show how

the equiangular spiral would appear. "Add another right triangle like this. Then add another and another and another. Just be sure to make each new leg the same size as the legs of the original triangle."

Sure enough, an equiangular spiral emerged, traced by the vertices of the triangles.

"That's fantastic!" the spider exclaimed. "But I have a question. What's a golden rectangle?"

"That's something to discuss another time," Penrose answered.

"In that case, I think I'll do my own mathematics with my web." And the spider returned to spinning its web.

What else is hidden in the golden rectangle?

If you look closely, you'll see lots of smaller squares and rectangles within each. In fact they go on forever. In other words there are infinitely many. And what is even more amazing is that each of the rectangles is itself a golden rectangle!

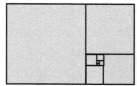

Historical Note: Golden rectangles have been known and used for thousands of years. They first appeared in the art and architecture of the ancient Greeks. Today, the golden rectangle is even used in the shape of a typical credit card.

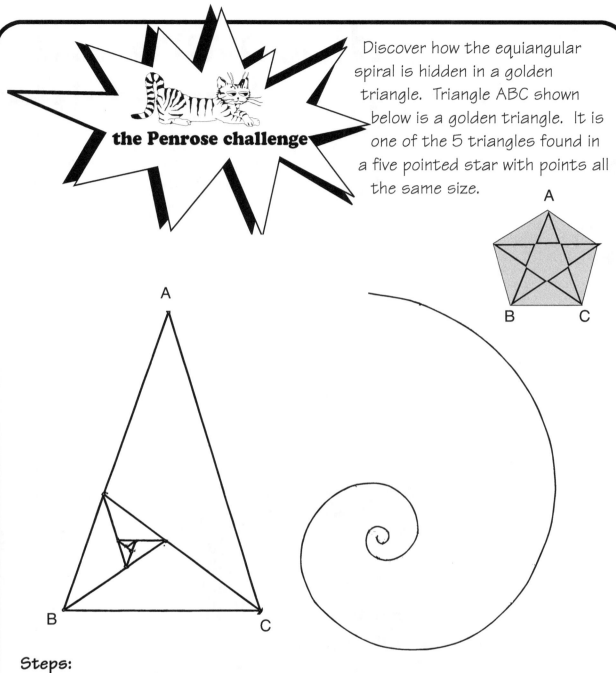

the Penrose challenge

Discover how the equiangular spiral is hidden in a golden triangle. Triangle ABC shown below is a golden triangle. It is one of the 5 triangles found in a five pointed star with points all the same size.

Steps:

1) Make a copy the equiangular spiral shown above.

2) Try to place it over triangle ABC so the curve touches the triangle's 3 vertices (A, B, and C).

3) Notice how the equiangular spiral also touches the vertices of all the smaller golden triangles within triangle ABC.

Solutions are in the back of the book.

Penrose discovers the mathematical rep-tiles

As the sun began to set, Penrose lay stretched out under the Adirondack chair in the front yard.

The moon was

begin-
ning
to
rise. It
was one of
those full
moon nights
and wild

creatures always seemed to be especially active during those nights. Penrose lay calmly taking in the changing light and watching the leaves fall to the ground. A quick movement caught his eye. "What was that?" he wondered.

He slowly crept over to have a closer look. He could not believe what he saw. A creature suddenly broke apart, and became four creatures identical in shape to the original one.

WOW!
What are you?

"Wow!" Penrose said, unable to contain his enthusiasm. "You are amazing."

"Who? Us?" one of them asked.

"Yes, you," Penrose replied. "What are you? I have never seen anything like that before."

"We're rep-tiles. Not your common everyday reptiles, but rep-tiles," one of them said.

"Tile as in tessellation?" Penrose asked.

"Exactly," a rep-tile replied. "Very good. Most creatures don't get it when we tell them."

"I have had training in mathematics from my mistress," Penrose said,

graciously giving her credit. "But how do you tessellate?"

"Actually we tessellate in reverse. We begin with a specific shape, and we figure out how to replicate that same shape and tile it within the original shape. Here is how it worked when you saw us." And the rep-tiles went back together to illustrate their point.

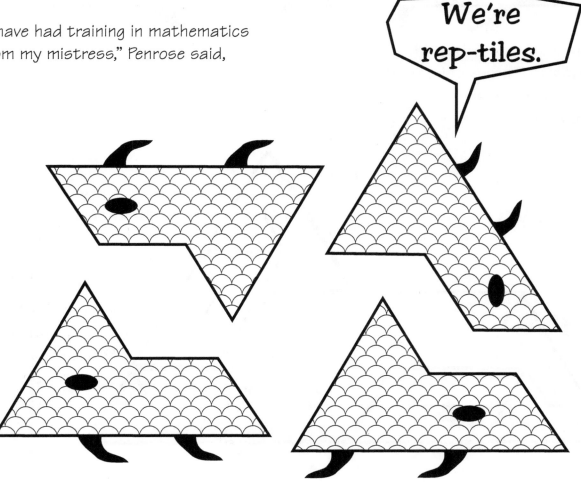

"Now we'll show you how we can continually replicate."

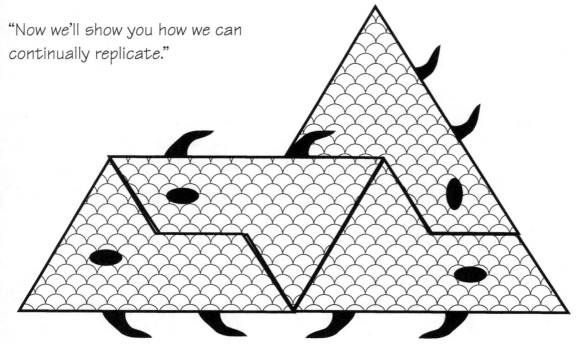

"That 's incredible," Penrose said, truly astonished. "Do any other shapes rep-tile also."

"You bet. Here is one for you to work on, but have to be going. We have lots more rep-tiling to do before the night is finished." With that the rep-tiles were off, leaving Penrose with this rep-tile puzzle to solve.

the Penrose challenge

Penrose's rep-tile puzzle

Using this shape, see if you can figure out a way to continually replicate it within itself.

See if your answer matches Penrose's in the solution section at the back of the book.

Penrose gets the prime numbers

"Why are you playing with those little squares, Penrose?" Maya asked condescendingly.

"I'm not playing, I'm making rectangles with them," Penrose replied, and demonstrated.

"I take twelve small squares of equal size.

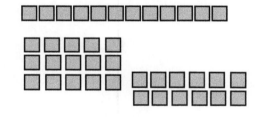

"Now, I arrange the 12 squares into different shaped rectangles.

"What do all these rectangles have in common?" Penrose asked Maya.

"I don't know," Maya replied, a confused look on her face.

"They all are composed of 12 squares, so each has an area of twelve," Penrose explained.

"That's obvious," Maya declared. "What's so great about that?"

"As you can see I formed rectangles like these below," Penrose illustrated.

"Each of these rectangles illustrates different factors for the number 12.

  1 & 12   because 1x12=12
  3 & 4   because 3x4=12
  2 & 6   because 2x6=12.

"So 1, 12, 3, 4, and 6 are all factors of 12, which means each divides into 12 with no remainder."

"So you use the rectangles to visualize the factors of 12," Maya interjected.

"Exactly!" Penrose exclaimed, happy to get his point across.

"Let me try one," Maya said.

" Okay. Take 5 little squares. How many different shaped rectangles can you make using all 5 squares?" Penrose asked with a smile on his face.

Maya thought and thought and thought, and finally said, "I get only one. Why?"

Let me try one.

"Don't be disappointed, one is correct

because 1 & 5 are the only factors of 5," Penrose answered.

"You've just discovered how to visualize a prime number. If the number of mini squares for the number can only be arranged to form one rectangle, as with the number 5, it shows that such a number's only factors are 1 and itself."

Okay. Let's see what you get using 5 little squares.

"So I can test if a number is prime by trying to form different rectangles," Maya shouted excitedly. "Let me test some more."

"Okay. Why don't you test — 7? 15? 18? 23?" Penrose suggested. "By the way," Penrose added, "A number that is not prime it is called **composite** because the number of squares can compose more than one rectangle."

*　　*　　*

Let me test some others.

What's the use of prime numbers?

Today prime numbers play a major role in keeping information private and secret when being transmitted over the Internet. Cryptology, codes, and ciphers depend on huge prime numbers to keep their secret.

Historical Note: Although computers have been programmed to find prime numbers, the sieve of Eratosthenes is a great way to find the prime numbers from 1 to 100. Eratosthenes was a Greek mathematician who lived from 275 B.C. to 194 B.C. This is the method he developed. When you finish, the diagram will have only prime numbers.

the Penrose challenge

The Sieve of Eratosthenes

Follow these steps to sort out all the prime numbers from 1 to 100 using Eratosthenes ' sieve method.

1) 1 is crossed out since it is not considered prime or composite.

1	2	3	4	5	6	7	8	9	10
11	12	13	14	15	16	17	18	19	20
21	22	23	24	25	26	27	28	29	30
31	32	33	34	35	36	37	38	39	40
41	42	43	44	45	46	47	48	49	50
51	52	53	54	55	56	57	58	59	60
61	62	63	64	65	66	67	68	69	70
71	72	73	74	75	76	77	78	79	80
81	82	83	84	85	86	87	88	89	90
91	92	93	94	95	96	97	98	99	100

2) Circle 2, the smallest positive even prime. Now cross out every 2nd number, these are all numbers with 2 as a factor.

3) Circle 3, the next prime. Now cross out every third number, these are all numbers with 3 as a factor.

4) Circle the next open number, namely 5. Now cross out every 5th number.

5) Continue this process until all numbers up through 100 are either circled or crossed out. The circled numbers are the prime numbers up through 100.

solution: Your sieve should have the following numbers circled-
2,3,5,7,11,13,17,19,23,29,31,37,41,43,47,53,59,61,67,71,73,79,83,89,97.

13

The day the numbers overpowered Penrose

It was a lazy summer day, and Watson and Penrose were stretched out in the backyard under the elm tree.

Watson could tell from the expression on Penrose's face that he was in deep thought about some math problem. "There you go again, working with numbers. Ever since I've known you, you have liked doing problems and puzzles. Have you always loved numbers?" Watson asked.

Penrose yawned, then replied, "No, not always. There was a time when I disliked numbers very very much."

> No, not always. There was a time I disliked numbers very very much.

"What? I can't believe that," Watson exclaimed, astonished.

"It's true. I was jealous of all the time my mistress spent working with numbers and on mathematics problems and ideas. I would go into her office on those days wanting attention, but she would be totally focused on her papers. She wasn't even aware I had entered. I would jump onto the desk and playfully nuzzle her free hand. No response. I'd try to play, but nothing. I plopped

onto her papers. That finally got her attention. 'No Penrose, I'm busy', she replied. I began to purr and push her papers. 'I'm right in the middle of my work. Not now, Penrose,' was her response."

"What did you do?" Watson asked.

"One day I decided to try to get rid of the numbers or chase them away. So when my mistress was gone, I went into her office. I entered slowly and stealthily. I realized I would have to confront them nose to nose, so I leaped onto her desk top. There on the top were tons of papers with numbers and symbols written all over them. Boldly, I raised my paw and began to move and mix the papers around the desk. Then, I began

pushing them off the desk to the floor even more boldly. Papers were flying all over.

'What's the big idea?' a voice shouted, startling me.

"I was so scared. I jumped to the floor. Papers were still floating down, but now the numbers were detaching themselves from the pages and coming down on me. Was I ever frightened!" Penrose declared, as he related his experience.

'Why are you mixing up the papers and pushing us down.' 3 asked.

'I...I...I was trying to get rid of you,' I replied.

"As I looked around I realized all the numbers from the pages were looking at me. Some were still on top of the desk, others were on the floor and some were floating down. I felt overpowered and outnumbered.

'Why are you trying to get rid of us? We haven't done anything to you,' the numbers shouted.

'My mistress pays more attention to you than to me,' I said sadly.

'Don't be a silly cat. Your mistress works with us. Granted, she loves working and discovering number ideas, but she cares deeply for you,' they replied sympathetically.

'Really?' I asked.

'Of course. If you take time to find out about us, you may find yourself feeling the same way she does about us. We haven't any intention of overpowering you. We'd like to help empower you even as we do with people,' 1 replied, speaking for all the numbers.

'What? empower? how?' I asked.

'Numbers are tools people use to make their lives less complicated,' 1 continued.

'Numbers seem to make things more complicated for me,' I replied.

'That is because you don't understand us yet. People keep track of things with us. We are the basic units of mathematics. We help measure things.

But why do cats and kids need or want numbers?

From the first time people made marks in the dust to count to the sophisticated calculations of today's computers, we have been there to help describe, keep track, measure, …have fun,' 1 said proudly.

'But why do cats and kids need or want numbers?' I asked.

'To learn, but also to have fun,' 2 said with a smile.

'What fun?' I asked boldly. And they began to show me all sorts of exciting things," Penrose said, ending his story.

"What fun did they show you that day, Penrose?" Watson asked, his cat curiosity having gotten to him.

"Let me show you a number trick," Penrose said.

the Penrose challenge

• Ask a friend to put a nickel in one hand and a dime in the other. Tell him or her to multiply the right hand's coin by any even number and the left hand's by any odd number and to add the amounts.

• Then ask for the answer. If the answer is even the nickel is in the right hand. If the answer is an odd number, then the dime is in the right hand.

How this works is explained in the solutions & answers section at the back of the book.

Penrose discovers a doughnut that is not for eating

"**W**hat in the world is she doing with that doughnut shape on her desk? Is it edible?" Penrose wondered aloud.

"Edible? I should hope not. And incidentally, I am NOT a doughnut," the shape shouted at Penrose. "I'm a mathematical object called a torus."

"Whatever you are, I still want to know why you are on my mistress's desk?" Penrose asked the object.

"I may be helping her solve a problem," the torus replied.

"Problem? What problem would have a doughnut for an answer?" Penrose asked.

"Please, not a doughnut— a torus. I don't call you stripes, so please don't call me doughnut," the shape insisted.

"Oh, sorry. I meant torus," Penrose said politely.

"Thank you. You asked to what problems I would be the answer. They'd be problems with which the usual Euclidean geometry shapes seem to be stumped. Do you know that there is more than one kind of geometry?" the torus asked.

"Of course!" Penrose said, trying not to seem ignorant. Unable to control his curiosity, he asked, "Well then, tell me more."

"Your world may seem to function just fine on a sphere with properties of Euclidean geometry, but the sphere and that geometry don't have all the answers," torus began to explain.

"All the answers?" Penrose questioned. "What do you mean?"

"Suppose I asked you what 6 divided by 2 is?" the torus replied.

"Correct. What about 12 divided by 0? What number is the answer to this?" the torus queried Penrose.

"No number I know," Penrose said with a puzzled look on his face.

"I would say 3," Penrose said.

"Right, and for 8 minus 0?" it asked.

"8," Penrose immediately replied.

"Precisely. There is not a single number from your world of numbers that can solve this problem," the torus explained.

"Well, what should we do?" Penrose asked.

"Look deeper, further...look out of the world of your numbers. But I did not ask you that problem to solve it with you, but to introduce myself as an answer to a mysterious problem." The torus tantalized Penrose's curiosity.

"What problem?" Penrose asked eagerly.

"The problem of the **The Three Paths & the Three Houses.** For each house three paths must be made — one to the well, one to the barn, and one to the woodshed. None of these paths must cross each other. Can you solve this?" the torus asked Penrose.

Penrose was perplexed. He thought... and thought... and thought...

thought... Suddenly his eyes began to gleam and he started to purr. "Now I know why you are more than a doughnut," he declared.

the Penrose challenge

Can you solve the problem of **The Three Paths & the Three Houses?**

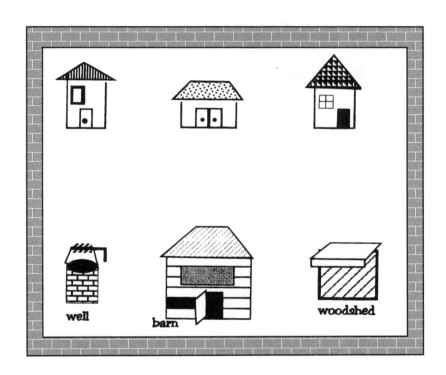

well   barn   woodshed

After you get your answer, see if Penrose's solution at the end of the book agrees with yours.

Penrose discovers the rods

Penrose was his usual mischievous self when he leaped onto his mistress's desk while she was out shopping.

It was his chance to snoop around, and see what she was up to.

"What are all these sticks piled on her desk?" Penrose wondered.

He saw columns of numbers with sticks laid out alongside them:

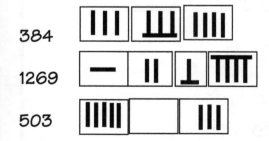

384

1269

503

72109 ?????????????

Penrose was in a playful mood. He couldn't resist batting some sticks around like toy balls, so he swatted a pile.

"Stop!" a voice shouted.

Penrose immediately stopped, his paw in mid-air. He realized the voice was coming from one of the sticks.

"What's the big idea, cat? Can't you see we're in a special order? Look what you did. You mixed my pile all up. I was the number 72,109," the stick sighed. "How will we get ourselves back in order?"

"Perhaps I can help," Penrose suggested.

"What can a cat know about numbers?" The stick said sarcastically. "Especially Chinese rod numerals."

"I've never heard of rod numerals," Penrose said.

"That's what I mean. How can you expect to help us?" the stick asked.

"But, I am a mathematically talented feline," Penrose countered. "So please explain," he asked.

"I don't know how to explain. We are just the rods, not the brains behind the numbering," the stick answered.

Penrose studied the column of numbers and rods, and thought, and pondered, and thought. The stick was beginning to get impatient and started to fidget.

"Well, let me study the layout of the other rods and their numbers," Penrose said as he stared at the numbers and their rods. "To straighten you back, I must figure out how your sticks have been set up for the number 72,109."

Then like a flash, Penrose raised his paw and said, "Don't be afraid, I believe I've have figured it out." And sure enough Penrose pushed the sticks around to form the rod numeral for 72,109.

the Penrose challenge

Discover Penrose's idea? Study each number and its rod numeral. Can you figure out how Penrose arranged the sticks to make the rod numeral for 72,109?

384	||| ⊔|| ||||
1269	— || ⊥ ⊤|||
503										
72109	? ? ? ? ?

Penrose's solution is given at the back of the book.

Penrose shares
some brain teaser puzzles

The mysterious dice puzzle

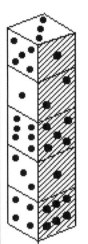

Here are five dice neatly stacked. You are allowed to view their faces from all sides, but you cannot touch the dice. Some of the faces of the dice are hidden in the stack. How many hidden dots (called pips) are there?

Penrose gives his answers at the back of the book.

Penrose's balancing act

How many pyramids will balance Penrose?

The knot puzzle

Take a piece of rope or twine. Hold one end in each hand. Can you figure out a way to tie a knot without either hand ever touching the end of the other hand's rope?

Penrose meets the mathematics actor x

"Will you please get off me,"

a muffled voice called out to Penrose, who was cat napping on some of his mistress's papers. A bit startled and still sleepy, Penrose stretched as he rose.

"Well, thank you! It was getting hard to breathe," the voice said.

Get off me.

"A talking x?" Penrose said, a note of disbelief in his voice.

"Well, you're a talking cat, why not a talking x?" x asked.

"What are you doing in my mistress's papers?" Penrose asked defensively.

"I'm helping her out with some problems," x answered.

" How can an alphabet symbol help her?" Penrose asked in disbelief.

Delighted at this opening, x said, "Let me tell you my story."

" You know, it took some time for me to become a popular letter, especially since I am near the end of the alphabet and there are very few words that start with x, except maybe xylophone and xerox."

"How about x-ray and xenophobe," Penrose interjected.

"Not bad," x replied, impressed by Penrose's words. "But let me continue. For some strange unknown reason I actually became a popular letter. Perhaps it was my shape or good looks. Eventually, I even became famous in such sayings as 'x marks the spot' on maps, 'sign on the line with the x' for contracts, and 'just put your x here' for people who couldn't sign their names. But never in my wildest dreams, did I ever believe I would play a role in mathematics, and be used to stand for a number. Imagine a letter, an alphabetical symbol, acting as a number.

It was unheard of. But that's what happened many many years ago, when some mathematicians chose x to help solve a problem."

certain problems, thereby making their work easier. You know how mathematicians love to use symbols, and seem to have their own language," x declared.

"How were you used?" Penrose asked, now very curious.

"Be patient. I'll explain," x replied. "I was chosen to stand for an unknown quantity."

"An unknown quantity?" Penrose blurted. "How could that help solve a problem."

" I was equally startled and surprised when it happened. A mathematician had stumbled on a new way to solve

"I've noticed ," said Penrose, "but the symbols make their work easier and shorter."

"Precisely why I was chosen," x responded quickly. " I remember that first problem very clearly, just as if it were yesterday: A certain number is multiplied by 6. The product is added to 76. Finally, you subtract 100 from this sum, and the result is 12. What number is this?"

"Wow, that's takes some thinking," Penrose replied scratching his head. "How did you help the mathematician solve this, x?"

"I am designated as the unknown which is to be found. A phrase of this problem is translated into a mathematical expression in which I appear. Most of the time you eventually end up with an equation. Here's how I work in the problem I told you.

First: A certain number is

multiplied by 6. This is written as 6x because 6x is one way mathematicians write 6 times x.

Second: The product is added to 76. This is written as 6x+76.

Lastly: You subtract 100 from this sum, and the result is 12. This is written as the equation:

$$6x+76-100=12$$

"That looks strange, but cool at the same time," Penrose said, "But what do you do with it?"

An unknown quantity? How could that help solve a problem.

I was equally startled and surprised when it happened.

X

28

"Since this is called an equation, both sides are equal to each other. So whatever you do to one side, the same must be done to the other. Otherwise, it won't remain an equation," x explained. "Mathematicians just undo everything that has been done to me, so the problem is solved when I stand alone. Let me show you. To undo subtracting 100, you do the opposite and add 100 to both sides. — $6x+76-100+100=12+100$ which becomes $6x+76=112$. Now undo adding 76 by subtracting 76 from both sides. We get

$$6x+76-76=112-76,$$

which becomes $6x=36$. To undo multiplying by 6, you do the opposite of multiplying and divide both sides by 6. This is $6x/6=36/6$, and now I stand alone as $x=6$—the answer to the problem."

"Wow! That was impressive," Penrose replied.

"You see Penrose, I think of myself as an actor. No, actually a superstar, who plays all these different number roles," x said proudly.

"Yes, but what do mathematicians call you?" Penrose asked.

"Mathematicians call me a **variable**, and they use that term for other letters, like y and z, which they also use for unknowns. Naturally I feel, since I was the first letter they used, they should have called us xariables. But, since that's not a word, and we do vary from problem to problem, I guess variable will do."

the Penrose challenge

Try using the variable x to translate these sentences into mathematical equations. Then try to solve them.

1) The sum of 23 and a number is 51. What's the number?

2) Twice a certain number is divided by 3 and added to 62, and this sum is 74. What's the number?

Penrose has his answers at the back of the book.

Graphing Penrose

Penrose leaped onto his mistress's desk.

As he looked around he got a startled look on his face. "Why," he thought aloud, "did she cut up my photograph?" He sounded so sad. "Was she upset I messed up her papers the other day?"

"Don't be a silly cat," called out the scissors lying next to the cut up photo.

Don't be silly cat.

"Talking scissors?" Penrose asked.

"It's no stranger than a mathematical cat," the scissors replied. "Your mistress didn't cut up your photo because she was mad at you. She is using its pieces as a model to introduce graphing to her class and to teach them how to read maps."

"Really?" Penrose asked, an incredulous tone to his voice.

"Really! Just read these instructions she wrote, and you'll see," the scissors reassured Penrose.

* * *

Graphs are used in many areas of our everyday lives. For example:

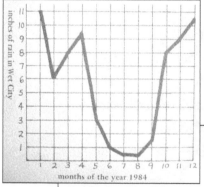

months of the year 1984

inches of rain in Wet City

- They give a picture of information that has been collected.

This graph collected information about how many inches of rain fell in different months of the year. Look at the 7th and 8th months. They had less than one inch of rain. How much rain did October have? Which month had 11 inches of rain? How many inches did April have?

April had 9 and a half inches of rain.
January had 11 inches of rain.
October had 8 inches of rain.

- They can be used to compare quantities as in bar and circle graphs such as those shown on the next page.

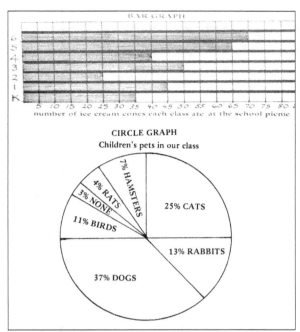

BAR GRAPH

number of ice cream cones each class ate at the school picnic

CIRCLE GRAPH
Children's pets in our class

7% HAMSTERS
4% RATS
3% NONE
11% BIRDS
25% CATS
13% RABBITS
37% DOGS

• Graphs are also used to locate places on road maps.

Road maps usually use a letter and number graphing method to show locations of places, such as cities and streets. On a road map each square has a letter and a number attached to it. If you looked up a street and it said it was located at C-3, that would mean you would find it somewhere in the square labeled C-3. To locate the square C-3, find where row C and column 3 intersect. The square where they meet is C-3.

How to do the Penrose puzzle graph

Draw the figure that appears in each square into its corresponding blank square grid. To find out, for example,

where to draw B-6, find the square below where row B and column 6 cross. When all squares are drawn in, you will have discovered the mystery picture. Another methods to use is to make a photocopy and cut out each picture square below and paste it in its corresponding location in the grid below it.

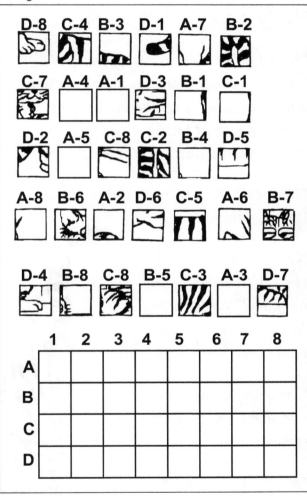

* * *

When Penrose finished reading his expression changed. A grin appeared on his face, his ears and tail perked up, and a loud purr could be heard.

It's time to operate

Penrose was in a very playful mood.

"Some days I feel like a kitten and want to do such things as bat falling leaves around or chase butterflies. Today is one of those days," Penrose mused to his cat pal Watson.

"Watson! Did you hear me? Watson!" Penrose called.

"What's up Penrose? Why all the shouting while I'm napping?" Watson asked. Watson got up and sauntered over to Penrose.

"I'm going to do some operations today," Penrose replied.

"What's that have to do with me?" Watson asked. "You're certainly not going to operate on me. I feel fine and I certainly don't need an operation."

"Don't be silly, Watson. I'm going to

do math operations," Penrose replied, laughing.

"What's a math operation?" Watson asked.

"Just imagine, Watson, numbers would be sitting around all day if it weren't for operations," Penrose said.

I'm going to do some operations today.

"You mean cutting numbers up?" Watson queried.

"No, no. I mean adding, subtracting, multiplying, dividing, squaring, cubing, for example. These are mathematical operations which you can do to numbers."

"Well, why didn't you say you were going to do some calculations in the first place?" Watson asked.

"Because these are called operations. But here's the catch, and where you come into the picture," Penrose explained.

"I am afraid to learn," Watson said hesitantly.

"Oh, come on. Surely I can interest you in a good tantalizing number problem — a problem where you can put your high intelligence to work." Penrose knew he could always influence Watson with flattery.

"Oh, all right, show me the problem," Watson replied, rising to the bait.

You're certainly not going to operate on me.

"Using numbers 2 9 6 5, in this order and any of the operation symbols, **+, −, x, ÷** , squaring etc. and an = symbol, and perhaps some parentheses, make this into an equation," Penrose asked.

"But these are just numbers. What do I do?" Watson asked.

"You put in symbols. For example, (2+9)-6=5," Penrose explained.

"Oh, that's what you want. How about this for a true statement, 2+9+6>5?" Watson said proudly.

"Not a bad idea. But that is not an equation," Penrose pointed out.

"I know that. I was just teasing you," Watson replied. "Give me another one."

"Try this. " Penrose wrote out 12 2 7 13 .

Watson thought, and thought, and thought. And finally a smile came across his face and he wrote (12÷2) +7=13.

"EXCELLENT," Penrose complimented Watson. "Here are some more for you and our readers."

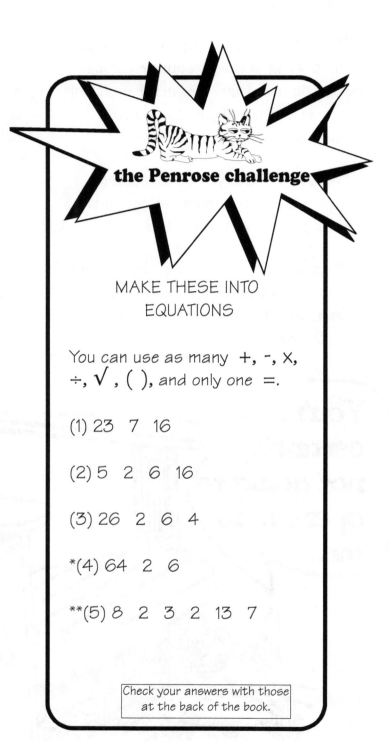

the Penrose challenge

MAKE THESE INTO EQUATIONS

You can use as many +, -, X, ÷, √ , ( ), and only one =.

(1) 23 7 16

(2) 5 2 6 16

(3) 26 2 6 4

*(4) 64 2 6

**(5) 8 2 3 2 13 7

Check your answers with those at the back of the book.

34

Penrose shoots for the stars

"**W**hat's this big star doing on his mistress's desk?" Penrose wondered.

Who's the star? The label read under the star. As he read further, Penrose discovered it was a solitaire game called **Shoot for the Stars.** "I love solitaire games," he thought as he read the following instructions.

Instructions

The five-pointed star, the pentagram, is the smallest mathematical star, and it is the grid for this game. As you see, it has 10 points of intersection — the 5 points of the star and the 5 vertex points of the interior pentagon.

   The object of the game is to cover any 9 of these points with 9 playing pieces, for which you can use pebbles, coins or even paperclips.

How to play:

1) Start by placing a piece on any empty point of the pentagram you want.

2) Move this piece through 2 consecutive points in a straight line. The 1st point may be occupied but the 2nd point (your landing point) must be empty.

3) Repeat steps 1 and 2 with a new piece.

4) See if you can become a star by placing all 9 pieces on the pentagram.

Penrose started a game. At first he was a bit frustrated, but finally he declared "I'm a star!"

Can you become a star?

Jelly beans teach Penrose how to estimate

"**D**on't just walk right by us!"

Penrose heard a faint voice as he walked by the large jar of jelly beans on the living room coffee table. He turned his head, and heard the voice again. "Yes, you! Aren't you the only moving thing nearby?" the voice continued.

"You're talking to me?" Penrose asked.

"Yes, indeed." the voice replied in a much louder tone. "Here, in the jar," the voice continued. "I am a jelly bean in the jar."

"I never heard of talking jelly beans," Penrose said.

"Well, I never talked to a cat before. So we're even," the jelly bean countered.

"Do you have any idea how boring it is to be stuck in this jar with these other jelly beans day in and day out while people come by and stare at

Don't just walk by us!

You're talking to me?

you with blank looks on their faces trying to guess how many of us jelly beans are in this jar?" the jelly bean asked.

"No! I had no idea you were in there feeling

36

so badly," Penrose said sympathetically. "But what can I do to help
relieve your boredom."

"For one thing, I guess we could
talk. But what could a jelly bean in
an estimating jar and a cat have in
common to talk about?" the jelly
bean wondered.

"First I visualize an easier problem, or
actually draw a
circle the same
size as the jar's
diameter. Now I
estimate how
many jelly
beans in a
circular layer.

> ## How about if I use my mathematical abilities?

> ## Mathematical abilities?

"What if I use my mathematical
abilities and help you estimate how
many jelly beans are in your jar?"
Penrose suggested.

"Mathematical abilities?" the jelly
bean questioned. "This should be
interesting— a cat with a talent for
mathematics. Tell me how you would
go about estimating. It can't be any
worse than some of the wild guesses
some people have made."

Suppose I figure 37. Now I must
estimate how many layers make up
the jar. I figure it is 11. So 37x11=407
would be my estimate for this jar,"
Penrose explained.

"Pretty clever," the jelly bean
conceded. "So for your estimates,
instead of making wild guesses, you
use logic and break the problem down
to smaller problems."

"That's right," Penrose replied. "Now let me reverse the tables on you, jelly bean. How many people do you guess are in this picture?"

"I am not bored any longer, just tired," jelly bean replied, and it quickly became silent and anonymous in the jar of jelly beans.

A CHALLENGE

What is your method of estimating how many people are in this drawing. What is your estimate? Good luck!

Penrose discusses his method at the back of the book, but get your answer before looking.

Penrose puzzles these out

Penrose's triangle puzzle

Can you make a triangle using three segments that are the size of these shown?

Show your solution or explain why it can't be done.

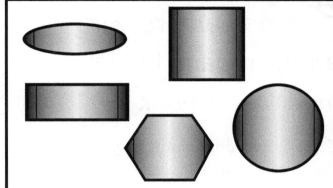

The sewer puzzle

Penrose wondered why the lids over street manholes are circular rather than square, rectangular, hexagonal or elliptical. Why are they only circular?

Solutions are at the end of the book.

The number puzzle.

(1) Choose a digit from 1 to 9 to occupy each square. You can use a digit more than once.

(2) The digits in each row, column and diagonal must total their end number.

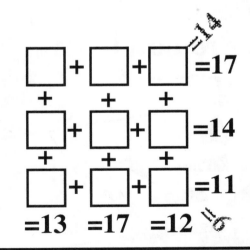

Penrose learns about congruent, similar & equal

Penrose sat reading an open page in his mistress's book —

"Objects are **congruent** if they are the same size and shape," the book said

"Well, why don't they just call them equal?" Penrose asked aloud.

"Because we're not!" replied one of the triangles from the page.

"But you are the same size and shape," Penrose argued.

"True, but in mathematics two objects are equal if they are exactly the same set of points. And although the other triangles and I are the same shape and size we occupy different points of the plane," triangle explained. "Look at these."

"I see," Penrose replied. "It is something like identical twins. They look exactly alike, but they are two different people."

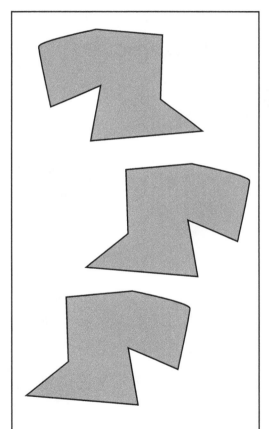

These three objects are the same size and shape, but do not occupy the same place on the plane. *So they are congruent but not equal.*

"Good analogy, Penrose," triangle complimented.

"Now, can you tell me how you can tell whether two objects are similar?" triangle asked.

"I think so," Penrose replied. "Similar objects are the same shape. This triangle, for example, has the same shape as you. So you're similar. Am I right?" Penrose asked.

"Absolutely! It is just a shrunk version of me. Now, Penrose, let's test your understanding. Can you pick out which of these sets of objects are congruent and which are only similar ?"

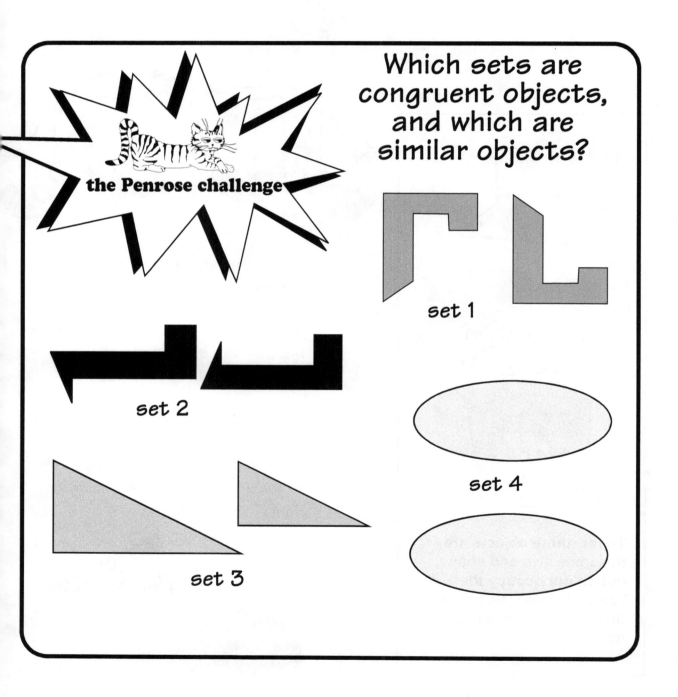

the Penrose challenge

Which sets are congruent objects, and which are similar objects?

set 1

set 2

set 3

set 4

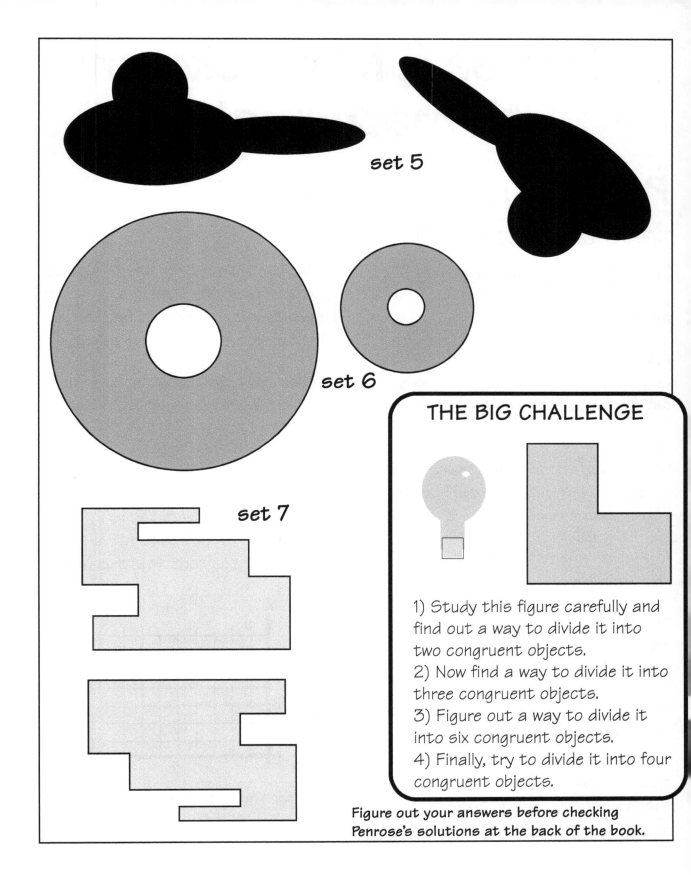

set 5

set 6

set 7

THE BIG CHALLENGE

1) Study this figure carefully and find out a way to divide it into two congruent objects.
2) Now find a way to divide it into three congruent objects.
3) Figure out a way to divide it into six congruent objects.
4) Finally, try to divide it into four congruent objects.

Figure out your answers before checking Penrose's solutions at the back of the book.

Penrose & Maya sketch with mathematics

Penrose had decided to be outdoors with his easel and paint brush.

He was concentrating on something very intently when Maya, the snoopy cat from next door, walked over to see what he was doing.

"What do all those numbers and dots have to do with art, Penrose?" Maya asked sarcastically.

"I'm painting a mathematical picture," Penrose replied.

"I should have guessed," Maya answered. "How can mathematics paint pictures?"

"Well, graphing is a way of picturing mathematics. Every mathematical equation can be pictured, and its picture is called its graph. And that's what I am doing," Penrose replied.

"It seems rather confusing, boring and stupid," Maya said in her imperious way.

"On the contrary," Penrose answered, rather irritated. "Making a mathematical drawing is fascinating. Ever read a map?" Penrose asked.

"Absolutely not! I don't need a map to tell me where I am going," Maya replied.

"Look. Since a map is drawn on a flat sheet of paper, every point or location on the paper can be described by a pair of numbers—one number for the horizontal axis and

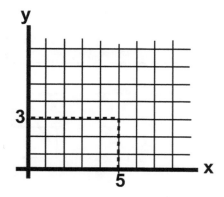

one for the vertical axis. The numbers (5,3) describe this point. First I find

44

5 on the horizontal axis and then 3 on the vertical axis and see where the two imaginary horizontal and vertical lines meet. That's the point for (5,3). Why don't you find the point (2,4) on my painting."

Maya was intrigued but didn't want to show it, so she simply raised her paw to the place she thought was correct. "There," she said, as she pointed.

I'm painting a mathematical picture.

(5,1) (7, 1/2) (9, 1/2)
(11,1) (12,4) (11,7)
(10 1/2, 9)   (9,10)
(8, 10 1/2) (7, 11 1/4)

What do all those numbers and dots have to do with art?

"Well, it is actually here," Penrose corrected.

"Why is that 4 and that 2?" Maya demanded.

"The point you located was for (4,2) not (2,4). Remember the order is very important. The first number is the horizontal number and the second is the vertical," Penrose explained.

"I see." This time Maya replied graciously. "But what do you do with all these points?"

"They give you a way of looking at mathematics as a picture, seeing patterns, solving problems. Besides it's fun to do," Penrose answered.

"FUN?" Maya questioned.

"Sure. Look at these

appear." Penrose held out a paper with many pairs of numbers.

"No way! How can numbers look like me and capture my beauty?" Maya asked.

"Mathematics has many tools that can be used to describe anything. And graphing is just one such tool. Why not see how mathematics pictures you, Maya?" Penrose asked.

Maya's curiosity got to her and she immediately began her mathematical portrait.

No way! How can numbers look like me and capture my beauty?

pairs of numbers I have been working on. If I graph them, a picture of you will

(5,1) (7, 1/2) (9, 1/2)
(11,1) (12,4) (11,7)
(10 1/2, 9) (9,10)
(8, 10 1/2) (7, 11 1/4)

the Penrose challenge

Can you discover what picture these numbers are hiding?

(5,1) (7, 1/2) (9, 1/2) (11,1) (12,4) (11,7) 10 1/2, 9) (9,10)
(8, 10 1/2) (7,11 1/4) (6,13) (5 1/2, 14) (5, 14 1/3)
(4, 15 1/2) (3 3/4, 14 1/2) (3, 14) (2, 12 1/2) (2 1/2, 12 1/5)
(3, 12) (3 1/2, 11 1/2) (3 1/2, 10) (4,9) (5,8) (5 3/4, 7)
(5 3/4,6) (5 4/5,5) (5 3/4, 4) (5,3) (6, 2 3/4)
(8, 2 1/3) (9, 2 1/2) (10,2) (9, 1 1/4) (8,1 1/8) (7,1 1/8)
(5,1)

• Get a sheet of graph paper. Graph and connect the points to see Maya's portrait. Be sure to connect the points in the order they are given.

A graph of this is given at the back of the book on the solutions page.

• Make your own drawing, and mathematize it into pairs of numbers which will produce a graph of it?

What's your conjecture?

"3, 5, 7, ?, ...
What would you guess comes after 7, Watson?" Penrose asked.

"How did you get that, Watson?" Penrose questioned.

"I simply looked at the numbers and noticed they were consecutive odd numbers, so 9 is the next consecutive odd number," Watson replied smugly.

You can't fool me Penrose.

What would you guess comes next?

3,5,7,?,....

"You can't fool me, Penrose. I've learned some mathematics from you. It's 9," Watson said confidently.

"That's a good guess. But what if I told you the next number is 11?" Penrose said.

"11!" shouted Watson. "Absolutely not. How could that be?"

"3,5,7 can also be thought of as the first 3 odd prime numbers, so the next odd prime is 11," Penrose replied.

"Sneaky!" Watson glared at Penrose.

"In fact, Watson, there is no guarantee the pattern is either 9 or 11. It could be something else," Penrose continued.

"What's your point, Penrose?" Watson asked.

"Mathematics deals with patterns which may lead us to conclusions," Penrose explained. "But there is no guarantee the pattern will always follow your conclusion."

"There isn't?" Watson asked.

"No. But the more information we have, the more we can test our conclusion. For example, let's say I gave you 2, 6, ... and asked what would come next. If the numbers go up by 4 it would be 2, 6, 10, 14, 18, ... But if the numbers are tripled each time it would be 2, 6, 18, 54, ... The more information we have, the better our guess," Penrose explained.

"So you are saying, don't jump to a conclusion," Watson said.

"Exactly. Get as much information as possible before venturing a conjecture," Penrose replied.

"A what?" Watson asked.

"A **conjecture** is just another word for guess," Penrose explained.

"I like that word. It has a good sound," Watson observed.

"How about making some conjectures on the patterns you see here?" Penrose challenged Watson.

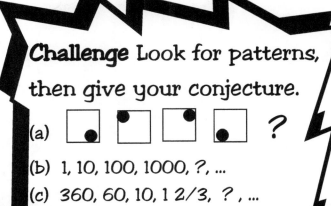

Challenge Look for patterns, then give your conjecture.

(a) ?

(b) 1, 10, 100, 1000, ?, ...

(c) 360, 60, 10, 1 2/3, ? , ...

(d) 2, 5, 6, 13, 14, 29, 30, ?

(e) What idea was used to arrange these nine digits?: 8,5,4,9,1,7,6,3,2 (very tricky)

Solutions are in the back of the book.

Optical illusions & Watson's close call

Penrose was basking in the summer sun drifting in and out of a cat nap dreaming he was the king of the jungle.

It was a perfect day for dozing.

SCREECH...CRASH...BARK...BARK...

Piercing sounds startled Penrose. "What in the world was that?" wondered Penrose, his fur standing on end. A few moments later he saw his friend Watson run around the corner looking very disturbed and rattled. "What happened to you Watson?"

"I just had one of the worst experiences of my life," Watson replied. "I was at the Murphy house and from a distance I saw a big dog in a cage. I felt safe walking by the cage, but as I approached the cage, the dog appeared outside the cage. It was just like magic. He came charging at me," recalled Watson. "I know he was in that cage. I saw him with my own eyes. What happened Penrose?"

"Well Watson, it seems that we cannot always rely on our eyes," replied Penrose. "I've looked through

many of my mistress's books on optical illusions. What you see there is often not real. In other words, in some cases you can't trust your eyes. We see things with both our eyes and our mind, and sometimes things get confused."

"How can that be, Penrose? I really doubt that," challenged Watson.

A bit irritated, Penrose continued, "Let me explain

screechh-hhhhhhh-hhhhhhh-hhhhh...

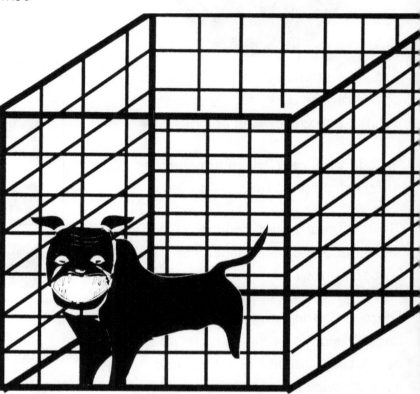

what happened with you and the dog. The sun and the shadows must have been at a perfect location, so as you stared at the dog your mind flipped the corners of the cage and placed

him inside the cage. If you had waited a little longer, perhaps you would have seen that he was really outside.

"Humph!" said Watson, skeptically.

"Our minds can even make colors seem to appear out of black and white," continued Penrose. Test it for yourself, Watson. Cut out the wheel shown here(next page). Now glue it on stiffer paper or cardboard. Stick a pencil in its center. Spin it with your paw. See how colors appear, Watson."

"My goodness, you're right Penrose. I see brown, and blue and other colors

51

too. How amazing! There are no colors on the disk, but by spinning it my mind produces the colors."

"In addition, each of us may see different colors," Penrose added.

"That's fascinating, Penrose. Can you show me some other illusions?" Watson asked.

Penrose nodded and continued. "The cage illusion is what is known as an oscillating illusion. Your mind and eyes go back and forth between different images. In your case, between the inside and outside of the cage.

"One of the first illusions in the study of optical illusions is this one. I'll call it the fabric illusion because it was first noticed as a design on some dress

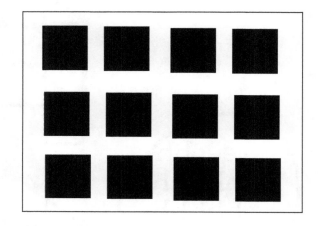

material. Notice how the lines appear to bend, even though they are straight.

"Now, here is a dot illusion. " Penrose said. "After staring at it for a short while, gray dots appear in the white area between the corners of the black squares."

"Truly amazing!" Watson exclaimed.

"There are hundreds of illusions, and many books written on them, Watson. Best you do a little studying next time you walk near a caged dog."

the Penrose challenge

When you look up close at this photograph made up of shaded squares, it's hard to tell what it is.

Step away from the photo, now what do you see?

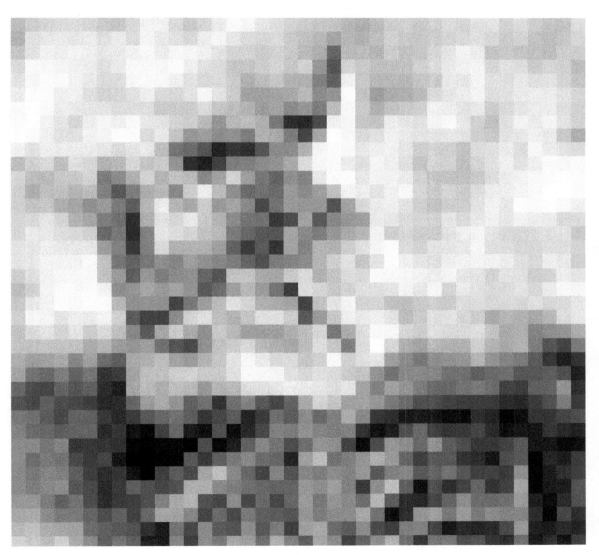

This is formed from a photograph of Penrose.

More optical illusion challenges

Study each diagram carefully and see if you can figure out the illusion it causes.

answers are given at the back of the book.

(1) What do you see?

(2) What do you see?

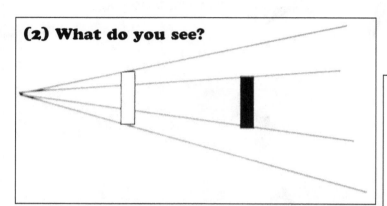

(3) What do you see?

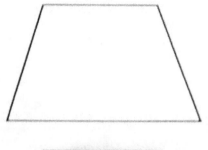

(4) What do you see?

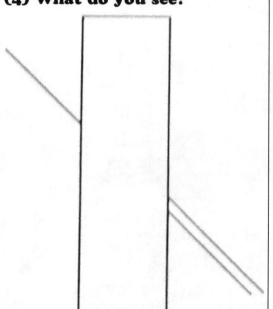

(5) What do you see?

SSSSS

Hint: Stare at the letters for a while, then turn the letters upside down. What do you notice?

Penrose adds them up

"**T**his is a strange assignment my mistress gave her students," Penrose thought as he punched buttons on the calculator.

"Here I am sitting adding the integers from 1 to 1000 on my calculator, and I might have already entered a number incorrectly," he complained as he added 127 to the previous sum.

"Stop!" 326 shouted.

"Now I'm imagining things again. I think numbers are talking to me."

"I am talking to you," 326 said. "Why are you doing this problem with a calculator?" it asked.

"You expect me to do it long hand using a pencil and paper?" Penrose countered.

"I expect you to do it the easiest way, and that means using your head," 326 replied. "And besides you might not always have a calculator handy."

"What do you mean?" Penrose asked.

Stop!

"Look. Lay out all the numbers like this," 326 explained, listing the numbers from 1 to 1000 in this fashion.

$$1 +2 +3+4+5+6+ \ ... \ +995+996+997+ 998 + 999+ 1000$$

"What good does that do?" Penrose asked, sounding a bit annoyed.

"Just be patient, and answer these questions," 326 continued.

$$1+2+3+4+5+$$

$$6+7+8+9+10+$$

$$11+...+990+99$$

$$1+992+$$

$$993+994+$$

$$995+996+997$$

- "What do you get when you add 1 and 1000?" "1001" Penrose answered.

- "What do you get when you add 2 and 999?" "1001" Penrose answered.

- "What do you get when you add 3 and 998?"

"1001" Penrose answered.

- "What do you get when you add 4 and 997?"

"1001" Penrose answered.

- "What do you get when you add 5 and 996?"

"1001" Penrose answered.

- "What do you get when you add 6 and 995?"

"1001" Penrose answered.

"I think I see what you're getting at," Penrose said. "Each successive number on the right is paired with one on the left, and they always total 1001."

"Exactly!" 326 said. "So what's the total"

Penrose thought for a moment, and started thinking out loud —"Since there are 1000 numbers, there must be 500 of these pairs. So the sum would be 500 times 1001, which is 500,500. That is cool!" Penrose had to admit. "And it saves a lot of time. And I bet this technique would work with other sums."

"You bet it does. Just remember to think about a problem and sometimes you can come up with a creative solution," 326 answered.

Try these out.

THE BIG CHALLENGE

Use the technique Penrose discovered to find the following sums:

1) Add up the counting numbers from 1 to 156.

2) Add up the counting numbers from 52 to 200.

Solutions are in the back of the book.

Penrose flexes the flexagons

"**I**'m not just any GON, like the hexagon, pentagon, and all those other polygons.

I'm a FLEXAGON. I'm mysterious," the strange object declared.

"Mysterious?" asked Penrose.

"Yes! In my folds I have hidden faces that come to view." With that comment the flexagon flexed itself, and a new face appeared with 3s on it.

"Wow, how did you do that?" Penrose asked.

"I'm a hexa-tetra-flexagon," it replied.

"That's a mouthful," Penrose said with a smile.

"**Tetra** stands for 4, and I have 4 edges. **Hexa** means 6, and I have 6 faces. Polygons only have two faces—one on the top side and one on the reverse side. But I have 4 more hidden within my folds. Make me and you'll find out how amazing I am."

* * *

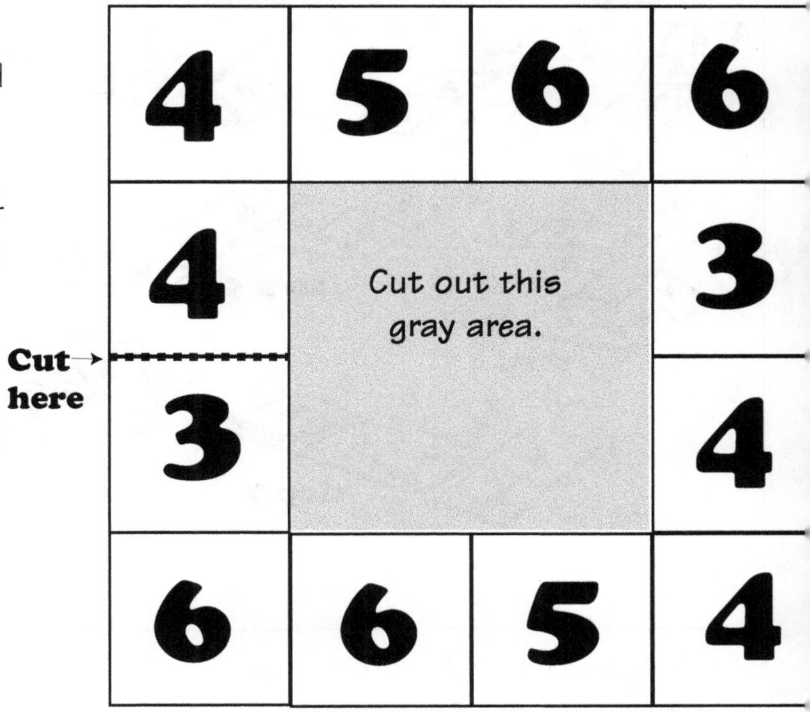

Here is how you can make a hexa-tetra-flexagon.

front side

4	5	6	6
4	*Cut out this gray area.*		3
3			4
6	6	5	4

Cut → here

back side

5	2	1	3
1	*Cut out this gray area.*		2
2			1
3	1	2	5

(gray border numbers: top 6, 5; left 6, 3, 4, 4; bottom 5, 6)

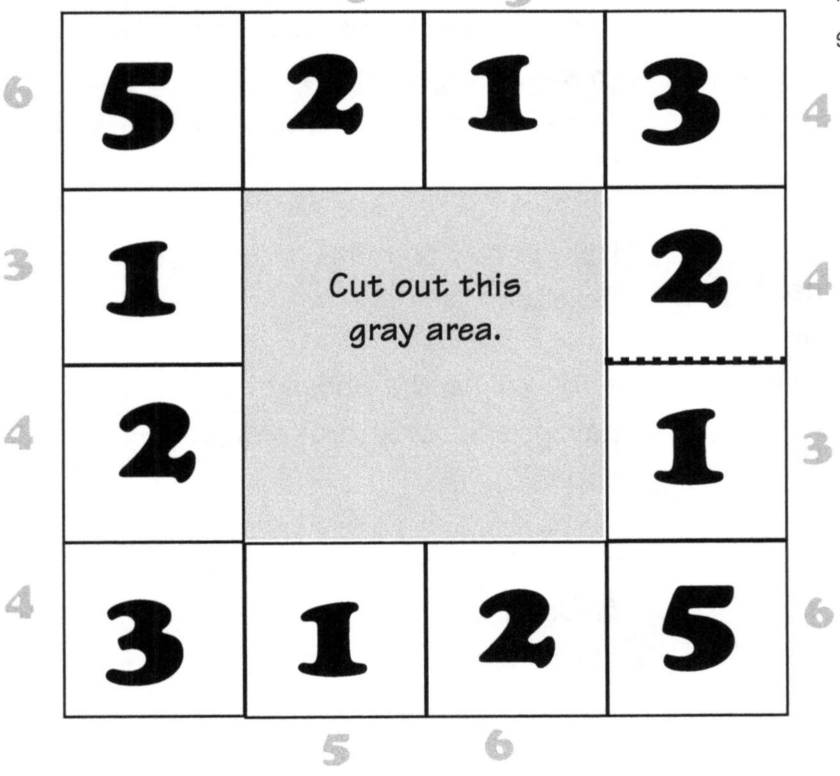

• Draw the squares and their numbers as shown on the front side above.

• On the back, place the numbers as shown on the left. Make sure that behind the 4 on the left top corner of the front side you write the 3 on the top right hand back corner.

(The gray numbers shown around the border of the back side are the numbers which should appear behind these on the front side.)

Now follow steps 1 through 9 on the following page.

59

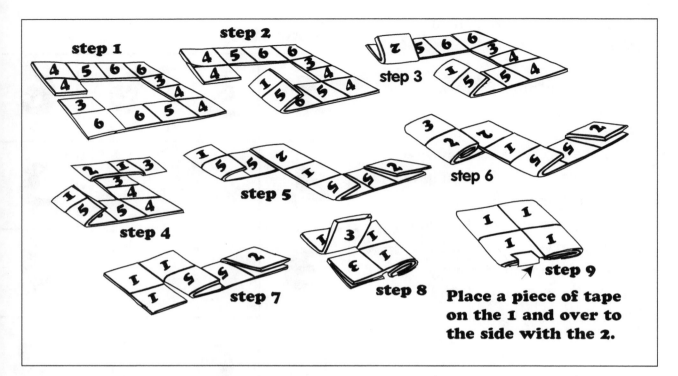

step 1

step 2

step 3

step 4

step 5

step 6

step 7

step 8

step 9

Place a piece of tape on the 1 and over to the side with the 2.

• To discover the hidden faces turn over the hexa-tetra-flexagon so all the 2s are on top. Fold along the vertical crease, and you'll find two new faces. Return to all 2s. Now fold along the horizontal, and discover two other hidden faces.

* * *

There are other types of flexagons. Here are some others you may want to explore at your local library or on the web.

tetra-tetra flexagon

hexa-hexa flexagon

tri-tetra flexagon

Here is one of Penrose's favorites because it is shaped like an ordinary piece of paper, but it is still mysterious. Its technical name is **tetra-tetra-flexagon**. The first tetra (meaning 4) stands for its 4 edges. The second tetra stands for its 4 flexing faces.

Here is how to make a tetra-tetra flexagon:

• You will need a sheet of paper, a pair of scissors, and a small piece of tape.

• Now follow these instructions and discover how the numbers get rearranged.

60

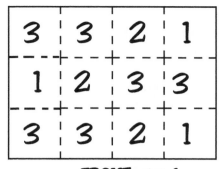

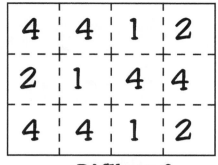

FRONT: step 1   **BACK: step 2**

Fold an 8 1/2 by 11 sheet of paper into 3 rows and 4 columns as shown. Number the creased boxes on the front and back sides as indicated.

step 3
• Taking a pair of scissors, cut the front as illustrated.

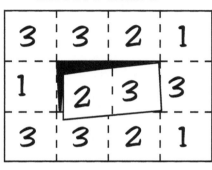

step 4
• Fold the 2-3 flap back as shown in this step.

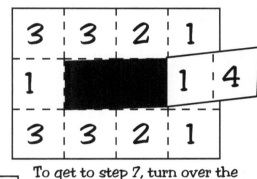

To get to step 7, turn over the flexagon after step 6. All 4s show up on the backside.

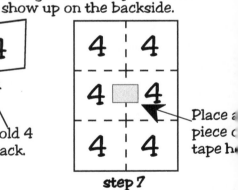

Fold 4 back.

Place a piece of tape here.

step 5   **step 6**   **step 7**

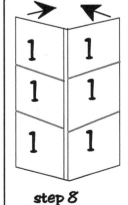

step 8

How to flex this flexagon:

When you get to step 8, you are ready to flex.

a) Crease on the vertical line and fold the 1s back.

b) Now open along the vertical and the 2s appear.

c) Repeat steps **a)** and **b)** above and the 3s will appear.

d) Reverse the steps in order to return to the original front and back faces of 1s and 4s.

There are many things you can do with this flexagon. You can use it to write secret messages which will be hidden on the inside parts. Or you might draw an interesting design on each side of the sheet of paper before cutting it, and then make the flexagon and see how the design changes as you flex the flexagon.

Penrose tells a snail about spirals

It was late afternoon and Penrose was relaxing in a box in the family room.

It was too beautiful a day to be indoors he thought as he looked out the window. Suddenly, he noticed a movement in the grass. He dashed outside and saw it was a snail crawling on the grass. He watched it slither along the grass, paying special attention to the curve of its shell. " I know that curve," Penrose thought out loud.

"Of course you do," the snail said, startling Penrose. "Aren't you Penrose the mathematical cat."

"Why yes, I am Penrose. I have seen your curve in my mistress's books. It is such a beautiful shape."

"Thank you. I think it is one of the best looking spirals around. Don't you?" the snail asked.

"It is not only lovely, it is so mathematical," Penrose replied.

"Tell me about my house," the snail asked. "I want to be informed."

"It is called an equiangular spiral. If I were to draw a radius from the center of your spiral, all the angles it makes along the curve would be the same size. And another of its special properties is that it fits perfectly into a golden rectangle. Here, let me show you how these properties look." Penrose sketched shapes in a bare patch of earth under the tree.

 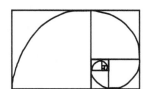

"Amazing. I like my home even more now," the snail replied.

"Perhaps we can meet again another day and discuss more mathematical ideas," Penrose hurriedly declared and dashed in to eat.

"I'd like that," the snail said as it continued along its path at a snail's pace.

* * *

I have seen your curve in many books.

"Peennnrossse. Here kitty ...kitty. Time for supper," his mistress called.

I think it is one of the best looking spirals around.

63

Here are some interesting things to learn and share with friends about spirals.

The Spiral Puzzle

Will your friends be tricked by Penrose's clever spiral puzzle?

What you need:

- a cord at least a yard or meter long.

- a push pin

What to do:

- Fold the cord so that one strand is longer than the other. In other words, do not fold it in half.

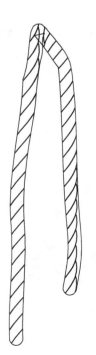

- From the fold point, A,

A

wind the cord into a spiral shape, as shown.

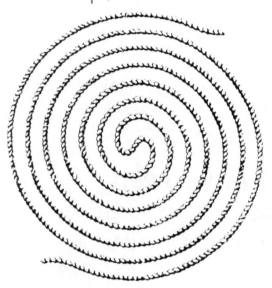

- Challenge your friend to find the middle and push the pin through the cord at that point.

- See how well your friend did by unwinding the cord from the spiral. In most cases the pin is off center.

the Penrose experiment

Here is something that looks like a spiral, or is it an optical illusion? To find out, trace some of the spiraling swirls using a crayon or marker. What happens?

Start tracing on this white line. Then try the one below it?

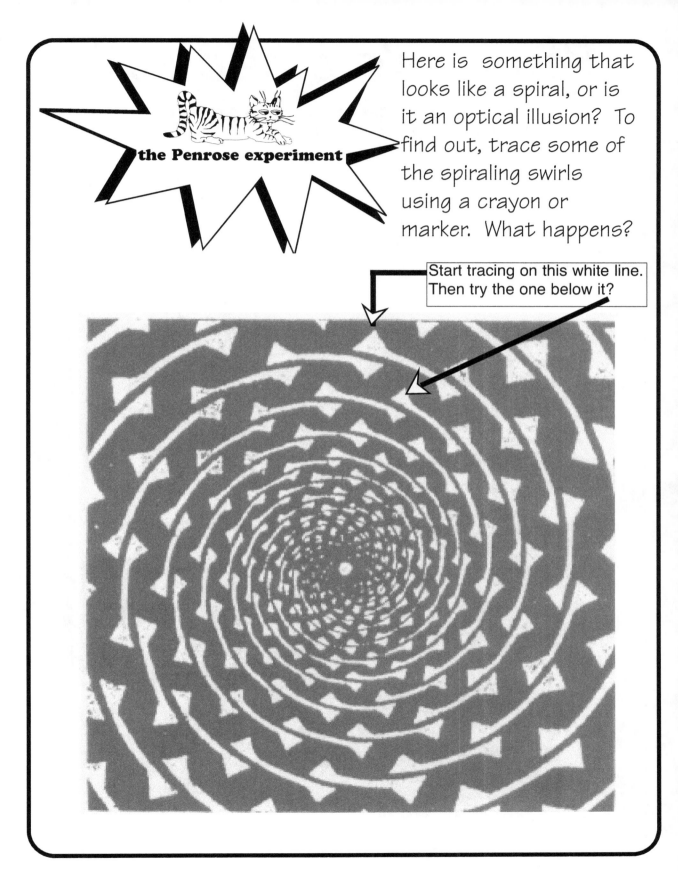

Penrose's close call with Probably

The first time Penrose met Probably was entirely by chance.

Dashing home to supper, Penrose literally ran into Probably. Penrose felt terrible he had not been more careful.

Penrose said, as he hurriedly tried to help gather the mess of things strewn all over the ground. Marbles, playing cards, dice and pennies were everywhere.

"I'm Penrose. I live a few blocks from here in the tan house."

"The probability of that statement being true is 1."

"What do you mean?"

"Hello, my name is Probably,

"Oh! I am so sorry I made you drop all your things. Here, let me help,"

and I would have guessed the tan house," Probably replied.

"Oh! How is that?" Penrose asked.

"My guess was between two houses, so that gave me a 50-50 chance of getting it right," Probably said as he bent over stuffing marbles back in a bag.

"Do you know much about the mathematics of probability?" Penrose asked, as he handed some pennies to Probably.

"They don't call me Probably for nothing," Probably bragged.

"Really?" Penrose sounded a bit amazed. "Is that what you are doing with all these things that spilled — probability problems?" Penrose asked.

"The probability of that statement being true is 1," Probably replied in a cryptic fashion.

"What do you mean?" Penrose's curiosity was aroused.

"Do you know what probability is?" Probably asked Penrose.

"YYYYYeeeeeessss, but why don't you start from the beginning," Penrose answered.

"**Probability** is a number that describes how likely a certain event might happen. For example, if I

dropped two pennies on the ground, what is the probability that both coins land heads up?" Probably asked.

"How do you calculate that probability number?" Penrose wondered.

"I am getting to that," Probably said. "My question was merely rhetorical. The way you find the probability of an event happening is by first listing all the possible events that can happen. The two coins can land in four ways—

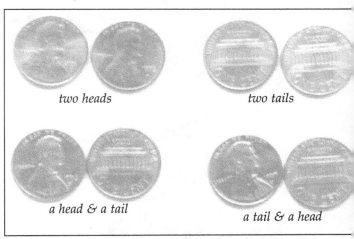

two heads   two tails

a head & a tail   a tail & a head

Then the probability of getting two heads is:

$$\frac{1}{4} = \frac{\text{how many ways two coins can land heads}}{\text{how many total ways the two coins can la}}$$

"I got it!" Penrose said excitedly. "So in that case, the probability of two coins landing with one a head and the other a tail is 2/4 which reduces to 1/2."

67

"Right on!" Probably exclaimed. "Let's see how you do with the bag of marbles. Inside I have 8 red, 4 blue, 6 green and 2 yellow marbles. If I asked you to reach in without looking and pick one marble, what is the probability of picking a red one?"

Penrose thought, and thought, and thought…then said, " 8/20."

But can you explain how you got that answer, so I know it was not a lucky guess?

"Exactly," Probably replied. "You are sharp, Penrose. But can you explain how you got that answer, so I know it was not a lucky guess?"

Penrose was a bit taken aback with that comment, but decided to be gracious and said, " The 8 is the number of red marbles in the bag. I could pick any of these. The 20 is the total number of marbles—all colors— in the bag. By the way 8/20 reduces to 2/5," Penrose replied.

"Great, but can you tell me the probability of not getting a red marble?" Probably asked, seeing if he could stump Penrose.

"Well, I'd see how many marbles are not red—the 4 blue, the 6 green and the 2 yellow—that is 12. I could pick any of these, so the probability of not picking a red is 12/20, which reduces to 3/5," Penrose said proudly.

"Now for the best part, Penrose. What does 2/5 plus 3/5 equal?" Probably asked.

"Why, 1," Penrose said, wondering why Probably asked.

"I know if I reach in and get a red or not get a red is a sure thing. Right?" Probably asked.

"Oh! I see. That explains your reply

earlier **The probability of that statement being true is 1'**," Penrose remembered. "It means it is sure to happen. There is no other possibility."

"Exactly! That was another way of saying it was true." Probably smiled as he spoke.

By now it was dark and each cat knew it would be missed at home, so they agreed to continue their probability work the next day.

Try these probability questions.

1) Make a cubic box. You can use this pattern if you like. Label the six sides with the numbers 1 through 6.

2) What is the probability of rolling this cube so that it lands with the 2 on top?

3) If you roll it 12 times. The two might come up __?__ times.

Roll it 12 times and see how many twos you get. Remember probability does not say it always happens that way, but that it is likely to happen in the long run. You may want to experiment with 36 rolls or even more.

the Penrose challenge

Fold into a cube as shown

| 1 |
| 2 |
| 5 | 3 | 6 |
| 4 |

BIG CHALLENGE:
What is the probability of not rolling a 2?

Penrose has his answers at the back of the book.

69

Penrose helps Sorry Snowflake

"Woe is me," lamented Sorry Snowflake.

Sorry Snowflake was the saddest of all snowflakes. It had lost its symmetry one very stormy night when a fierce wind took it by surprise and tore off some of its parts. Without its symmetry, it is teased mercilessly by the other snowflakes. "You are a sorry example of a snowflake," they taunted it. "In fact, you don't even look like a snowflake. So don't even call yourself a snowflake anymore." They would go on and on teasing Sorry Snowflake for hours.

But Sorry Snowflake did not give up hope, because it felt that under the right climate conditions its missing parts might grow back. But as more and more time passed the more discouraged it became. Finally it couldn't control its sorrow. "Woe, woe, woe is me," Sorry cried. Its cries were so loud that Penrose, who had

gone outside to check on the weather for a moment, heard the cries and looked up.

Woe is me.

"What's the matter?" Penrose asked sympathetically.

"It's been a long time and nothing has grown back," Sorry replied.

70

"Grown back?" Penrose asked in a puzzled tone.

"Yes," Sorry began to explain. "I used to have perfect symmetry, but climate conditions destroyed my symmetry. I was hoping crystals would grow back. But now look at me," Sorry said crying.

"Don't cry. I am sure I can get help to fill in the gaps. I know snowflakes are lovely delicate objects that have what is called **hexagonal symmetry**. That means you have 6 lines of symmetry, like a hexagon. An object has **symmetry** if you can find a line that divides it into **two identical parts**. So all we have to do is draw in your 6 lines of symmetry and make mirror images of the designs on opposite sides of each line. This should fill in your lost parts."

"Brilliant!" shouted Sorry. "Please proceed."

Help Sorry Snowflake by drawing in its missing parts, and make Sorry Snowflake just Snowflake again.

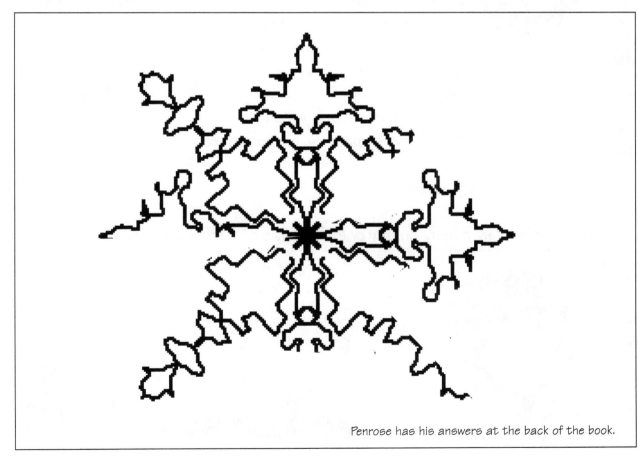

Penrose has his answers at the back of the book.

71

Penrose continued teaching Snowflake about what he had learned about symmetry from watching his mistress work. "You know Sorry. Oops! pardon me, you're not Sorry Snowflake any longer. Anyway, symmetry is a beautiful phenomenon that occurs in many objects in nature. It's not just in you, Snowflake. Look at a butterfly, an insect, a flower and the human skeleton—all possess symmetry," Penrose explained. "That's fascinating" Snowflake called back as it floated away happy to be complete. Penrose heard Snowflake saying "Thank you Penrose" as its voice faded. "Good-by Snowflake," Penrose called back.

Even though Penrose felt sad to see Snowflake leave, he continued to think about the beauty of symmetry. "Some objects have only one line of symmetry and others many. But there are also many things in nature which do not possess symmetry. For example, look at a pepper, an amoeba, a mountain range, clouds—none of these have symmetry."

butterfly

amoeba

beetle

pepper

Draw in lines of symmetry on any of the pictures of this page that have symmetry.

half an orange

mountain range

the Penrose challenge

1. Write out the English capital letters of the English alphabet. Study them carefully and decide which have either a horizontal, vertical or no line of symmetry by trying to cut them into two identical halves with either a vertical or horizontal line.

- Which letters have vertical lines of symmetry?
- Which have horizontal lines of symmetry.
- Which have both vertical and horizontal? Which have none?
- Decipher this secret message by using the idea of lines of symmetry for the letters to fill in the parts of the letters missing.

CAN YOU READ
THIS MESSAGE?

2. Draw in all the lines of symmetry you can find for each of the four objects shown here.

Penrose has his answers at the back of the book.

73

Penrose shares his favorite math magic tricks

"**N**ow what?" Watson asked as he settled down in Penrose's living room.

"Math problems strewn all over the rug, a top hat and wand. You're in big trouble if your mistress comes home now."

"I'm just studying her latest work, and you'll be amazed at what I discovered."

"I'm sure I will be," Watson said as he yawned. Math wasn't his favorite thing.

"Listen Watson, I'm talking magic...math magic," Penrose shouted.

"Really? Show me," Watson replied skeptically, but perked up.

"I've gone through these papers. There are so many great tricks here. Where should I start?" Penrose thought out loud.

"Start with your favorite ones," Watson said as he settled down on the bookshelf for the show.

Penrose began and with each trick Watson's eyes got bigger and bigger. "Wow! How did you do that?" Watson asked eagerly.

"It's all in the math," Penrose replied, then bowed, and walked away as Watson chased after him.

Here are some of Penrose's favorite mathemagics tricks.

Really?

George Washington flips over mathematics trick

- Take a $1 bill. The front has a picture of George Washington.

- Fold the bill in half lengthwise by folding the top down, as shown.

- Now fold this in half by folding the left side to the right side, as shown.

- Now unfold the bottom part of the folded bill to the left.

- Now open the top half up. What happened to George Washington?

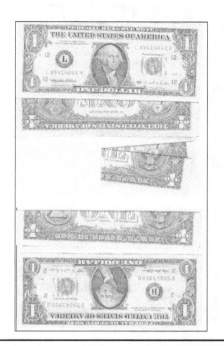

The astonishing number trick

752

- Ask a friend to pick any three digit number which has different digits in the one's and hundred's place. For example, 752

257

- Then, ask your friend to write the number in reverse order so the one's digit is the hundred's, the ten's is the ten's and the hundred's is the one's. 257

495

- Now tell your friend to subtract the smaller number from the larger number. 752-257 = 495

- Finally ask your friend to tell you the digit that is in the one's place. 5

Knowing this single digit, you can tell your friend, what the final number was. How?

5

In the final number, the one's and the hundred's digits always total 9 and the ten's digit is always 9. For our example, the final number was 495. Your friend would tell you 5, which you then figure makes the hundred's digit 4 since 4+5=9. And we know the ten's digit is always 9. Therefore, the final number is 495.

example:

5763

1387

2449

3029

2976

8612

6970

4236

7023

6070

49995

Penrose's super add it trick

Ask a friend to select and write five 4-digit numbers in a column. Now you write below these your five numbers, which you will choose in a very special way. Draw a line under the 10th number, and astound your friend by immediately adding up the 10 numbers.

The secret to this trick lies in how you choose your five numbers. Choose your numbers so that each of your friend's numbers plus one of yours total 9999. For example, for 5763 you would put down 4236 because 5763+4236= 9999. This means the ten numbers total would be the same as adding 9,999 five times. You can do this quickly in your head by thinking of 9,999 as 10,000-1. So the answer will be 50,000-5 or 49,995.

You can change the trick in various ways. Make the numbers your friend puts down longer or shorter numbers. Do not specify how many numbers your friend must put down. Just say, write down as many 4-digit numbers as you like. If they put down six the total will be 60,000-6; for seven its 70,000-7. For five 3-digit numbers it would be 5,000-5.

To keep your friend from discovering your method, it's a good idea to mix up the order of the numbers you put down.

Penrose's birthday trick

Take your birthday. →

Example: March 13. Since March is the 3rd month, the number for of this date is 313.

Multiply the month's number by 5. → **3 x 5=15**

Add 9 to this product. → **15 + 9=24**

Multiply this sum by 5. → **24 x 5=120**

Add 11 to this product. → **120 + 11=131**

Multiply this sum by 4. → **131 x 4=524**

Add the day's date of your birthday. → **524 + 13=537**

Subtract 224 from this. The result will always be your month and day of birth. → **537 - 224=313**

The birthdate we started with in its number form.

Penrose draws the magic line

Ask a friend to pick any two numbers, and write them in a column. Say they choose 21 and 2.

Next, ask them to add more numbers, but in a special way— by always adding the total of the two previous numbers.

21
2
23
25
48
73
121
194
315
624

Now ask them to draw a line after any number on the column. You can immediately total the numbers above the line by simply subtracting the second number from the top of the list from the second number below the line (315 - 2 = 313).

Penrose hears about how the solids got sliced

"So you're taking some ZZZZZs, and cat-napping again Penrose," cube said, nudging Penrose whose eyes were at half-mast.

"I thought I would take a little sunbath on this beautiful day," Penrose replied.

"Would you like to hear my scary sunbathing story about the day

Sure.

slicer came into town?" cube asked.

"Sure," Penrose said, remembering the exciting story cube had told him about spheres.

*   *   *

The slicer, as the plane was sometimes called, was in town. But why? What brought the slicer to Solidsville this time? The last time it was here it transformed a cube into many pyramids by passing through it at different angles.

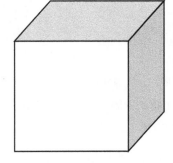

Would you like to hear my scary sunbathing story?

Slicer walked slowly into the general store. A small unsuspecting solid behind the counter asked, "May I help you?"

"Why, yes! thank you," the slicer

answered in a pleasant voice, which made all the other solids in the store turn to look. They had only heard bad stories about the slicer. Could this be THE slicer they had heard about?

"I'm looking for the five Platonic solids," the slicer continued. "I have a few surprises for them."

Meanwhile, at the country club the Platonic solids lay basking by the pool. It was one of those lazy summer days, and they had decided to take a pool break before getting back to the business of finding the best and most efficient way to pack solids in a rectangular container.

"Well, hexahedron," tetrahedron addressed cube.

I'm looking for the five Platonic solids.

They are all together at the country club.

"They love surprises," the small solid replied. "Today they are all together at a meeting at the country club down the road."

"Thank you," the slicer replied and headed in that direction.

As slicer walked, the solids scattered and cut a wide swath for it to pass.

* * *

Tetrahedron was very formal and could never bring itself to call hexahedron by its nickname, cube. "I have been thinking about mixing certain solids when packing them."

"I thought we had all agreed to take a break from work and just relax. Let's not talk shop," cube replied, half asleep.

At that moment slicer entered the pool area. All of the Platonic solids were suddenly attentive, except cube, who had fallen asleep.

"Whaaaaaaat are you doing here, slicer?" tetrahedron asked in a timid tone.

"No fooling around," cube replied, its eyes still closed. "You can't frighten me with that old joke pretending the slicer is here."

"It is not a joke," slicer replied.

At which cube leaped off of its lounge, recognizing slicer's voice.

"What do you want?" cube asked, trying not to appear frightened.

"I've come to truncate you," slicer replied.

"We are really fine just as we are.... I don't plan to do any traveling. ...I don't need a trunk.... As you know my faces are identical squares, all my angles are right, my edges are all congruent and I have eight vertices. I certainly don't want an elephant trunk for a nose. I am just fine," cube replied.

"Exactly my point," slicer began. "You Platonic solids could use a change.

It's about time you experienced a new look. Just relax," slicer continued.

"No, please, not me again," cube pleaded.

"Don't be frightened, cube. You know it doesn't hurt, and it isn't permanent. It is like getting a new

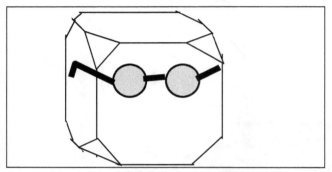

hair style," slicer tried to reassure cube. And with that comment slicer, the plane, moved so swiftly that all 8 corners of cube were cut off. The other Platonic solids were in a state of shock. They couldn't believe how cube looked. They couldn't help it, but they began to laugh. Slicer turned toward icosahedron, and they all became quiet. "Don't you think cube looks intriguing now?" slicer asked. "Oh yes," they all replied.

"Well then, let's give all of you a new look too." And with that comment, slicer transformed the other four Platonic solids into their truncated versions, so each corner appeared to be cut off and flattened.

* * *

"Wow! That is a great story," Penrose told cube.

"I could see you liked it. You never dosed off once," cube replied.

"Cube, I never knew anything about truncating. But why do it?" Penrose asked.

"Have you ever seen the facets of a crystal with all its faces? That's what truncating does. A cube has 6 faces. But, when I'm truncated at my 8 vertices, I suddenly have 8 more faces. Truncated, I look more intriguing. The more faces a crystal has the more ways it can capture light. Look at this picture of a crystal."

"It's beautiful! Wow, the light passing through it changes colors," Penrose said in wonder.

"That's another story, Penrose. I'll let you get back to your sunbath," advised cube walking away.

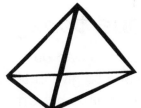

the Penrose challenge

Truncate each of these five Platonic solids and discover their new look.

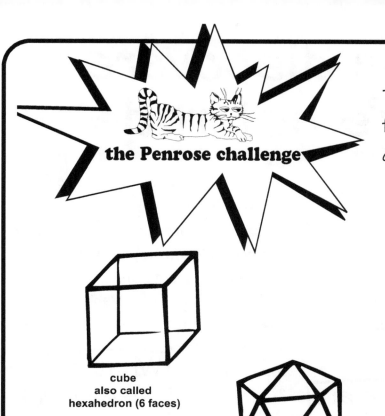

cube
also called
hexahedron (6 faces)

tetrahedron (4 faces)

icosahedron (20 faces)

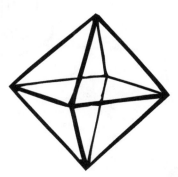

octahedron (8 faces)

dodecahedron (12 faces)

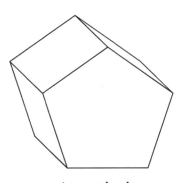

pentagonal prism.

NOTE: Any solid can be truncated by just snipping off each of its corners. You may want to trace each one. Then with an eraser get rid of their corners, and sketch in what is left.

Penrose has his answers at the back of the book.

Penrose discovers Napier's hot rods

"Penrose felt especially mischievous today.

He knew his mistress was out, and it was a perfect time to give in to his curiosity. He crept into her office, eager to see her new project.

not write the numbers on paper?" he asked out loud.

"Because we are not just sticks with numbers. We are **Napier rods** — developed by Scottish mathematician, John Napier in the late 16th century," the rod with the number 2 at the top said.

> We are Napier rods

> What are these sticks with numbers?

Leaping onto her desk, he found a pile of sticks. "What are these?" thought Penrose. "Sticks with numbers. Why

"You're that old?" Penrose asked, astonished.

"We may be over 500 years old, but

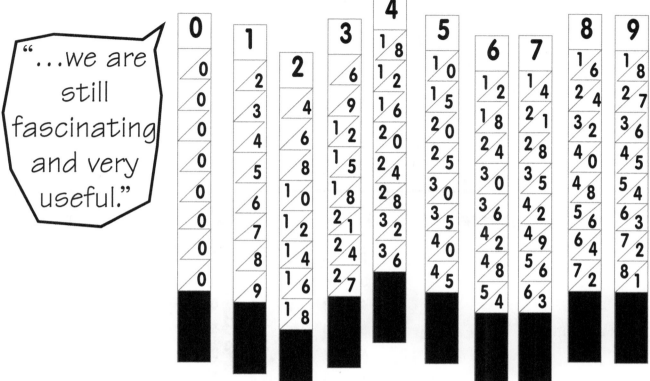

we are still fascinating and very use-ful," all the rods declared in unison.

"Useful?" Penrose asked.

"Indeed!" the 2 rod replied. "Look, if I am placed along side the 6 rod, like this— you can think of us as the number 26, and can use us to multiply 26 by 1, 2, 3, 4, 5, 6, 7, 8, or 9."

"That sounds great, but how do I do that?" Penrose asked.

26

"Suppose you want to multiply 26 by 8. You simply put the 2 and the 6 rod side by side, like this. Then count down to the 8th row from the top. Here you find 1/6 (on rod 2) and 4/8 (on rod 6). Now all you have to do is add these numbers in a special way.

$$\begin{array}{r} 16 \\ + 48 \\ \hline 208 \end{array}$$

Notice that the bottom numbers are placed one space over to the right before adding.

"So you are a type of ancient calculator," Penrose said.

"We like to think of ourselves as **Napier's hot rods**. Merchants and sailors in the 1600s carried a set of us, just as many people today carry around a hand calculator," they said proudly.

"Exactly!" Penrose exclaimed. "You are great! Would you mind if my readers tried a few problems with you?"

"We would be proud."

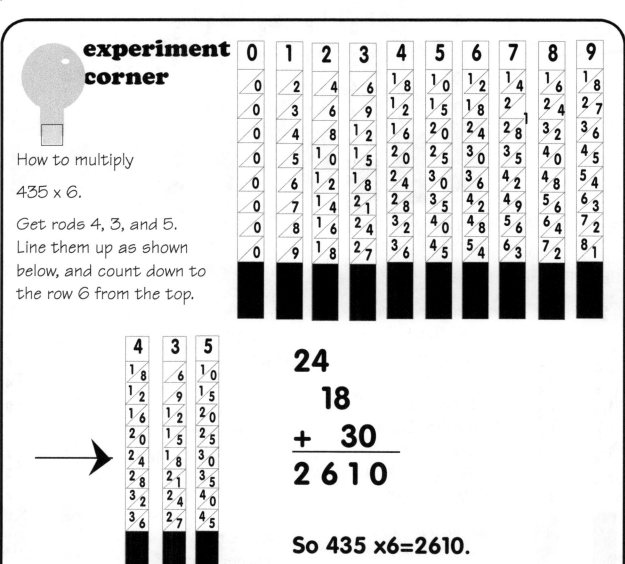

experiment corner

How to multiply

435 x 6.

Get rods 4, 3, and 5. Line them up as shown below, and count down to the row 6 from the top.

24
18
+ 30
2 6 1 0

So 435 x6=2610.

the Penrose challenge

Make a set of Napier rods by copying the ten rods shown on page 86 on ten strips of paper. Or you may want to make a photocopy of the rods and cut them out.

CHALLENGE:
Try your Napier rods on these problems. You can check you steps and answers at the back of the book.

(a) 38 x 6

(b) 5 x 8

(c) 127 x 9

These two problems are BIG CHALLENGES.

*(d) 95 x 64

(e) 123 x 57

If you get stuck on (d) and (e), I give some hints below.

*Try breaking up the problem into two problems.
First do 95 × 6, and then 95 × 4.

Penrose tackles mazes

On this particular day Penrose's mistress was working a maze a friend had given her.

Feeling a bit ignored by her inattention, Penrose ran over and plopped down on her papers and began to nonchalantly lick his paws. He knew his mistress was irritated by his interruption, but he pretended not to notice. He pushed her pencil with his paws, trying to endear himself. She carefully lifted him from her work and lay him next to her— petting him all the while.

Penrose thought—"Oh, it is one of those work days. I guess I'll have to amuse myself with my own maze." In his mind he created a giant cat maze. He pretended he was captive in its middle, and had to find his way out. Can you help him?

Penrose actually was having more fun with mazes than he realized. In fact, here are some mazes he found for you to enjoy doing.

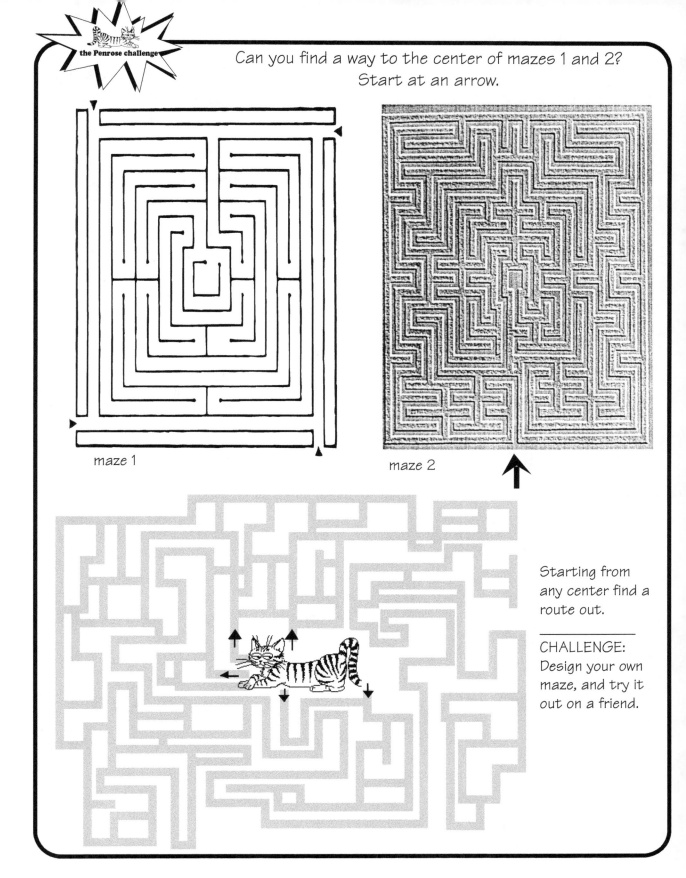

the Penrose challenge

Can you find a way to the center of mazes 1 and 2?
Start at an arrow.

maze 1

maze 2

Starting from
any center find a
route out.

CHALLENGE:
Design your own
maze, and try it
out on a friend.

Penrose crosses π's path

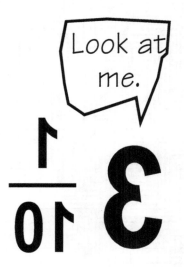

Look at me.

$\frac{1}{10}3$

I can do better than that.

$3\frac{7}{50}$

It was a glorious sunny day.

Penrose headed for his favorite spot—the third terrace in the backyard. It always caught the morning sun full force. As he settled down, and was just beginning to drift off, he heard voices.

"Look at me," $3\frac{1}{10}$ said.

$$3\frac{1}{10} = \frac{31}{10} = 3.1$$

"Well, I can do better than that," $3\frac{7}{50}$ said,

as it proceeded to convert itself to a decimal.

$$3\frac{7}{50} = \frac{157}{50} = \frac{157}{50}\frac{\times 2}{\times 2} = \frac{314}{100} = 3.14$$

"That is nothing compared to what I can do," $3\frac{705}{5000}$ said. "Watch this!"

$$3\frac{705}{5000} = \frac{15705}{5000}\frac{\times 2}{\times 2} = \frac{31410}{10000} = 3.141$$

"What are they doing?" Penrose wondered aloud.

"They are trying to capture me," a voice said.

Startled, Penrose turned and found the symbol π which he had seen many times written in his mistress's notes.

"What are they doing?"

"They are trying to capture me."

a fraction," π said proudly. Turning to Penrose, it asked, "And do you know why?"

"Why?" Penrose asked.

"I am the illusive number π," the voice explained. "Hey! You mixed numbers might as well give up. I've been prodded, poked, and stretched out to millions of decimal places by the best minds. The ancient Greek Archimedes used $\frac{22}{7}$ for me, but it wasn't exact. In ancient China, Ch'ang Hong tried to say I was $\sqrt{10}$, but that wasn't so. There's no end in sight. None have been able to turn me into

"Because I'm an irrational number," π said.

"What does that mean?" Penrose asked.

"I cannot be written as a fraction," π replied. "It has actually been proven. In fact, some math enthusiasts have been entered in the Guiness Book of Records for memorizing me to over 5000 decimal places. But, I just go on and on. I have fascinated mathematicians for centuries. They have devised all sorts of complicated methods to figure out my never ending non-repeating decimals, and now with super computers to do their computations, you can view me to nearly a billion places."

Suddenly, behind π a string of numbers appeared. It was π's never ending non-repeating decimals.

It shows how you were first discovered thousands of years ago," Penrose explained.

" $\dfrac{C}{d}$?" π asked.

Penrose continued, "Yes, **C** stands for the circle's **circumference** (the distance around the circle), and **d** is its **diameter** (the distance across the circle). Just imagine every circle's circumference divided by its diameter equals you, π. No matter how small or how enormous the circle is."

"I never knew that," π said, an amazed note in its voice. "That makes me even more special."

"I guess we both learned something today," Penrose said and began to purr.

"But," Penrose began to say.

"But what?" π interrupted him.

"I've seen you expressed in the fractional formula — $\dfrac{C}{d}$.

Check it out for yourself. Does any size circle's circumference divided by its diameter equal π? EXPERIMENT'S STEPS:

the Penrose experiment

(1) To do this experiment you will need a string and a ruler.

See what you find out?

(2) Wrap a piece of string carefully around each circle drawn here so the string's length will be approximately equal to its circumference.

(3) Measure each string's length with your ruler.

(4) Use your ruler to measure each string's diameter.

(5) Now divide each circle's circumference you measured by its diameter.

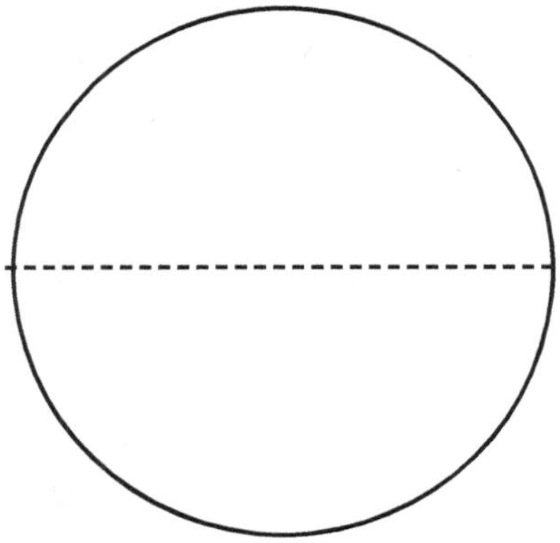

C: circumference_____

d: diameter _____

C divided by d: _____

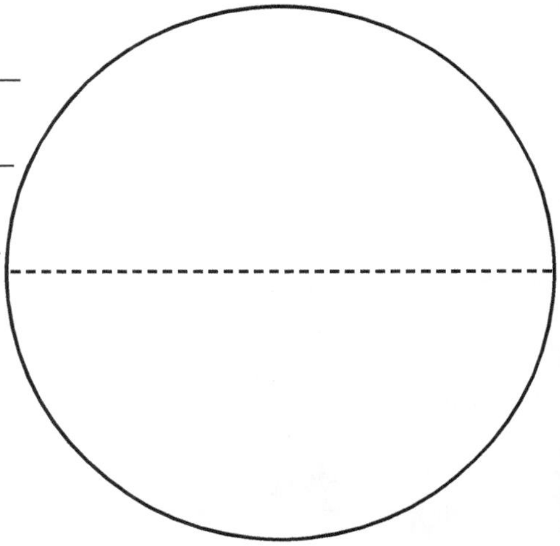

C: circumference_____

d: diameter _____

C divided by d: _____

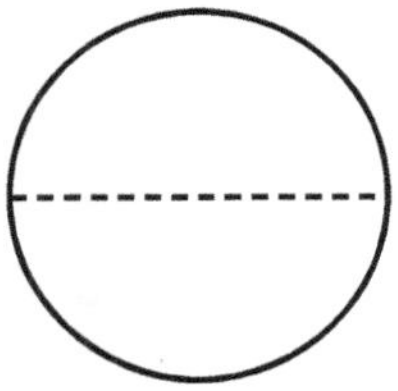

C: circumference_____

d: diameter _____

C divided by d: _____

In each case the circumference divided by the diameter is equal to 3 and a little bit more.

93

Watson & Penrose are at it again

"**P**enrose you are at it again…math, math, math," Watson teased Penrose.

"Watson, I am having a great time learning this new game. Math is not all problems and computations. I thought you would have at least learned that from all our conversations," Penrose countered.

"What new game?" Watson asked, changing the subject.

"You want to try it with me?" Penrose asked.

What new game?

"Welllllll…" Watson hesitated.

"You will love it," Penrose immediately interrupted. "Look, I have 13 crayons fanned out. But you can play it with pencils, small sticks, whatever you have available," Penrose explained.

"Where did you learn about this game? And what's it called?" Watson asked as his cat curiosity began to take over.

"I've talked to you about the great puzzlist Sam Loyd?" Penrose replied.

"Wait a minute I thought this was a game and not a puzzle," Watson said.

"Don't worry, Watson. Calm down. It is a game. He also invented games. But games involve strategy. And strategy involves logic. And.."

"And logic means mathematics is in the picture," Watson said filling in Penrose words.

"Okay, I guess you did get the message," Penrose replied. "So do you want to play?"

"Sure, let's go for it." Watson said with an excited tone to his voice. "This time I'm challenging you."

Sam Loyd's Petal Game

Get 13 crayons, pencils, small sticks — whatever you have available. Arrange them as shown in the diagram.

RULES:
• Alternating turns, each player can take 1 or 2 adjacent pieces at a time.

• The player removing the last piece is the winner.

Remember, you can take 2 playing pieces only if they are adjacent to each other with no blank places between them.

Can you figure out how the second player can always win?

Add more playing pieces and ask another player to join you. It will definitely complicate your strategy.

What's with the bugs

A pesky buzzing noise kept interfering with Penrose's reading.

"I wish that bee would buzz off so I can read!" Penrose declared. Then Penrose looked up and discovered what all the buzz was about.

Laboriously, but without complaining, the orb spider put in the last filament of its web. "Another magnificent web," the spider boasted. "A mathematical and artistic feat!"

"Always blowing your own horn," the honeybee buzzed at the spider. "You're not the only show in town. People always wonder how I am able to tessellate these hexagonal cells

Another mathematical and artistic feat.

for my honey. How I chose the hexagonal shape over the cube and equilateral triangular shapes."

"Exactly!" the spider chimed in. "Just look at my web and you'll find chords, radii, the idea of parallel, an

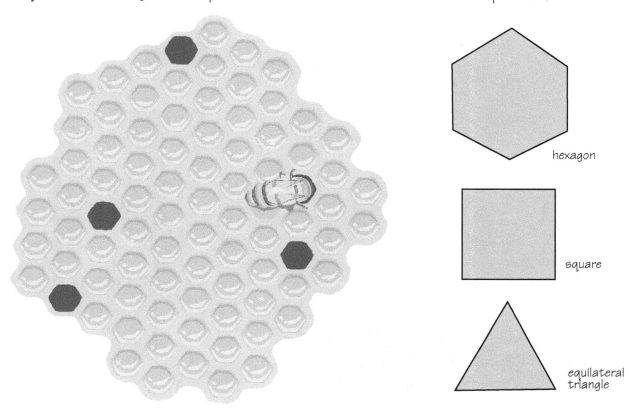

hexagon

square

equilateral triangle

"That, I am sure was an accident," the spider teased.

"Accident, my antenna. I used mathematics to figure out that the hexagon shape would hold more honey while using less wax to form the cells," the bee explained proudly.

"There you go again with your mathematical honeycombs," chirped the cricket. "You two are always bragging about the mathematical ideas in your structures," it countered.

equiangular spiral and even the number **e** and the catenary curve I am told."

"Show me where those are," demanded the bee.

"I would be glad to if you would just come over here on my web," the spider said, trying to entice the bee.

"No way!" said the bee, "I can see quite well from here."

"Oh, all right," the spider conceded, and climbed along its web pointing out chords used to form the ever growing equiangular spiral. "See, the

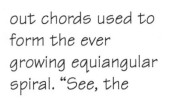

Ha! I use mathematics to make my honeycomb.

You two are not the only ones who use mathematics in your structures.

chords stacked between two radii are parallel. My web is an approximation of an equiangular spiral, where the angles formed by imaginary tangents are equal in size. And when the morning dew hangs on the chords of my web, I am told they are transformed into catenary curves. The equation of such a curve uses the transcendental number e. And..."

"Just one minute," the bee interrupted. "Don't say another word, I believe you, even though I haven't the foggiest idea what it all means."

"It simply means," the cricket jumped in, "that mathematics appears in nature. How it describes nature can be complicated, but for sure it's there."

"You're right about that," spider agreed.

"In addition," the cricket explained, wanting to challenge the spider's and the bee's boasting, "Have you ever looked at the geodesic-like eyes of dragonflies, the sym-metry of a butterfly, or the code dance you bees do when you return to the hive to tell the other workers where you found nectar. Even the origin of the word beeline comes from the fact that you bees instinctively know the geometric principle that the shortest dis-tance between two points is a line."

The spider and the bee were dumfounded and astonished by the cricket's knowledge.

"Incidentally, it is believed that the number of cricket chirps is mathe-matically tied into the surrounding temperature," the cricket said, with a big smile on its face.

"It is? I mean, it is." The bee suddenly caught itself, but decided to keep its ignorance to itself, "I must buzz-off to the hive."

"And I must work on my web some more," the spider declared, dashing off along its web.

The cricket hopped off, happy to have put an end to their endless bragging.

Here is a glimpse at how a dragonfly sees through its geodesic-like eyes.

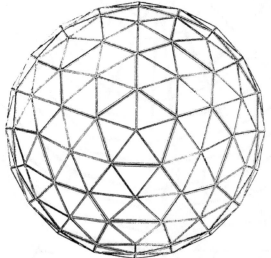

Here is an example of a geodesic structure, somewhat like the structure of a dragonfly's eye.

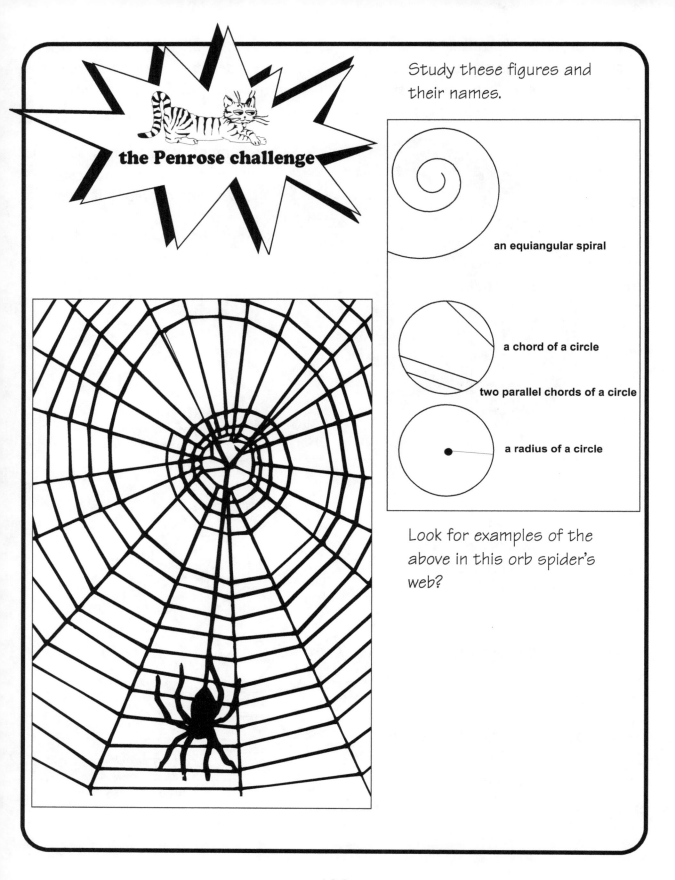

the Penrose challenge

Study these figures and their names.

an equiangular spiral

a chord of a circle

two parallel chords of a circle

a radius of a circle

Look for examples of the above in this orb spider's web?

Penrose puts his logic to work

"These puzzles are too good not to share," Penrose thought as he worked and worked on them.

Try them out for yourself.

The coin puzzle

These eight silver coins look identical except one is slightly heavier because it is counterfeit. Using a balance scale, what is the least number of weighings you would have to make to find which coin is counterfeit?

Measuring time puzzle

Suppose you have these two glass timers. One is a 9 minute timer and one is a 17 minute timer. How can you use them to measure 25 minutes.?

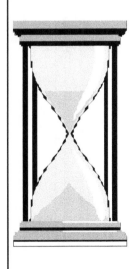

The four 5s puzzle

Using any of the four operations, +, −, ×, ÷ and parentheses make these four 5s come out to be 100?

5 5 5 5

The triangle puzzle

1. Toothpicks were used to form these 8 triangles. Remove six toothpicks and end up with 2 triangles.

2. Now, using the original figure, remove four toothpicks and end up with 4 triangles in which each toothpick is a side of a triangle.

Laying the squares puzzle

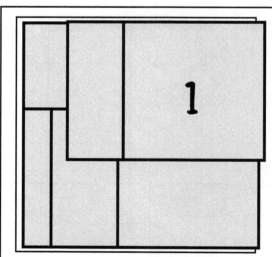

Six congruent squares are laid one on top of another as shown. The top square has the number 1 on it. Number the other five squares in the reverse order they were laid down.

Solutions are at the back of the book.

1+1 ≠ 2 ????? Penrose's question

"What do you mean 1+1 doesn't equal 2?" Watson fired at Penrose.

"Calm down Watson," Penrose said in a quiet voice. "You might learn something new. I know I did when my curiosity got the best of me."

"Oh, you and your curiosity. All right, let's hear it," Watson said, challenging Penrose.

"Listen, Watson. It's true 1+1 equals 2, but it can equal 10 also," Penrose replied.

"10?" Watson questioned, feeling exasperated and skeptical.

"Sure," Penrose countered with his usual confidence.

"How! Prove it." Watson said impatiently.

Calm down Watson. You might learn something new.

103

"If you think of 10 in a different number system," Penrose blurted out, then continued, "rather than the system we usually use. You know, base 10 is not the only way to count. The Babylonians used base 60."

"60...that's crazy," Watson exploded, not able to control himself.

"Yes! Check it out." Penrose challenged. "And for your information, the Mayan used base 20, and when the concept of numbers was just evolving, people didn't even have number systems. They just tallied amounts with their fingers, in the sand or dust, and even with notches etched in bones or sticks," Penrose explained. "If you look at the binary numbers, rather than base 10 numbers, you'll..."

Watson interrupted Penrose abruptly, "I don't get this stuff."

"Give me a chance," Penrose

continued. You'll discover that in the binary system numbers are written using powers of 2, rather than powers of base 10. The placevalue of each place is:

$$\ldots \quad \underline{16} \quad \underline{8} \quad \underline{4} \quad \underline{2} \quad \underline{1}$$
$$2^4=16 \quad 2^3=8 \quad 2^2=4 \quad 2^1=2 \quad 2^0=1$$

"So to write 7 we would use 1-four and 1-two and 1-one, making the number 111 for 7."

"Why can't you just use 7-ones, like we use in base 10?" Watson asked, sounding bewildered.

"Because base two, also called the binary system, uses only 2 numerals to write numbers—the numerals 1 and 0. That's why it's called bi(two)-nary," Penrose explained.

"That seems like a silly way to write numbers," Watson replied. "What good are these binary numbers anyway? They just confuse me."

"They are invaluable to computers and digital technology," Penrose

Listen, Watson. It's true 1+1 equals 2, but it can equal 10 also.

answered. "You wouldn't have that portable digital CD player and headphones over your ears, if it weren't for base 2. We wouldn't be able to program and communicate instructions and data to computers, if it weren't for binary numbers," Penrose tried to explain.

"Please explain how do 1s and 0s speak to computers?" Watson asked in a curious and now polite manner.

10?

"See Watson, electricity is the key. It powers computers, and is either **on** or **off** —there are only two possibilities. Circuit boards—making up the system in computers— are composed of the microchips. These are laid out with gates(also called transistors) which either let electricity pass through or not (it's 'on' or 'off') — these '**ons**' and '**offs**' are translated into 1s and 0s. All numbers are written using strings of 1s and 0s, and all words also have their unique strings of 1s and 0s— their own pattern on a circuit board," Penrose explained.

"That's amazing. But I'm still a bit confused. Perhaps I'll just learn how to write numbers in base 2 for starters," Watson announced.

* * * * * * *

Penrose said, "I saw an easy way kids were using their fingers to write the numbers from 1 to 31 in base 2. They wrote the number 16 on their right thumb, 8 on their index finger, 4 on their middle finger, 2 on their ring finger, and 1 on their baby finger. Then, when they wanted to write, say 13, they would simply stare at those fingers and see which combination totaled 13—index, middle and baby. Each of those gets the 1 digit and all the rest get 0. So 13 is 1101 in base 2. Try some on your own Watson."

the Penrose challenge

If each of our ten fingers stands for a base two placevalue numeral, then their placevalue labels would be 1, 2, 4, 8, 16, 32, etc.

(1) First, finish filling in the ?s on the left hand with their base 2 placevalue.

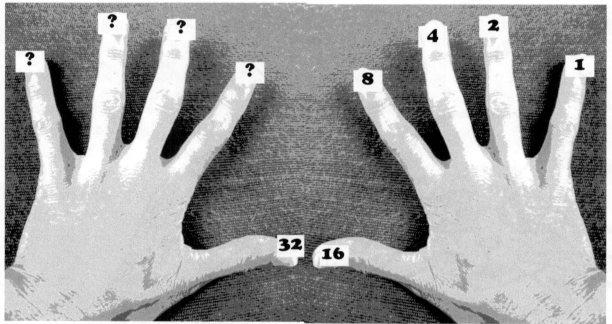

(2) Using this information, figure out what would be the largest binary number your ten figures could represent.

(a) Write it in base 2?

BIG CHALLENGE: How would you write 5, 16 and 11 in base 2?

Check your answers with those at the back of the book.

Penrose shares his solitaire-game puzzles

"I am bored, bored, bored," Maya declared.

"Let it not be said I am closed minded. Let me try them." Maya began doing the solitaire-game puzzle. Before she knew it she was really into it.

Penrose watched, and a big grin came across his face. "The solitaire-game always does the trick," he thought to himself.

*   *   *

Here are the solitaire-games he gave Maya, why not try them out yourself?

"Do you know what I do when I feel bored?" Penrose asked.

"I am afraid to ask." Maya replied sarcastically. "What?"

"I like to do a solitaire-game puzzle," Penrose said with a smile on his face.

"A game-puzzle? You have got to be joking," Maya said, sounding bored.

"You can at least be open minded. Will you give them a try?" Penrose asked her calmly.

A Solitaire Game of Numbers

Object: Make an equation using $+$, $-$, $\times$, $\div$ and an $=$ from three numbers which are in consecutive squares. The sample at the right shows some moves.

6 +	7 =	13	27 ÷	3
10	25	5	30	9
28 −	7 ×	4 =	28	56
20 =	8	15	10	19
4	11	9	3	5

continued on next page—

Now see how many equations you can come up with on this board of numbers

3	7	12	23	8
10	20	5	30	6
28	7	4	60	56
20	5	15	10	19
4	11	9	3	12

 Make up your own board of numbers, and give it to a friend.

Moving the Tower of Cards

STAGE 1 (beginner game):

Make three cards with the numbers 1, 2, and 3 written on them as shown.

Arrange the cards in descending order on space A.

Following the rules below, find a way to move the stack from space A to space C

Rules:

1) A larger valued card may never be placed on top of a smaller valued card.

2) You can only move one card at a time to a new space.

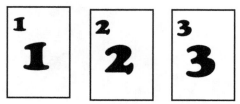

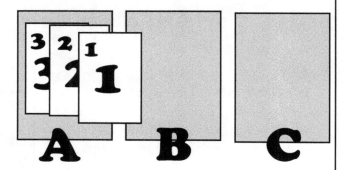

STAGE 2 (intermediate game) :

Make four cards with the numbers 1, 2, 3 and 4 written on them, and move the stack from A to C.

STAGE 3 (advanced game) :

Make five cards with the numbers 1, 2, 3,4 and 5 written on them, and move the stack from A to C.

solutions
& answers
section

solutions & answers section

page 5_____

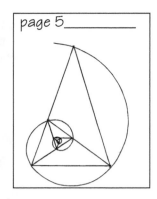

page 9_____

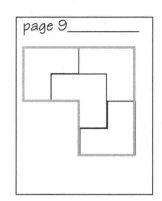

page 17_____

A nickel is 5 pennies and a dime is 10 pennies. So a nickel represents an odd number, and a dime represents an even number. Whenever you multiply an even number by any number its product is always even. So the hand with the dime will always make an even number. But when you multiply an odd number by an even number the product is even, and when you multiply an odd number by an odd number the product is an odd number. So its the hand with the nickel that will vary. If you add two even numbers, the sum is even. If you add an odd and an even number, the result is odd. **So if the answer is even, the nickel is in the hand which was multiplied by an even number, which was the right hand. If the answer is odd the nickel is in the hand which was multiplied by and odd number, which was the left hand.**

page 21_____

The problem cannot be solved on our spherical world unless we used tunnels. But if the world were in the shape of a doughnut (a torus) the paths could be drawn without crossing each other from each of the houses to the well, barn and woodshed as shown.

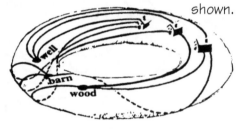

page 24_____

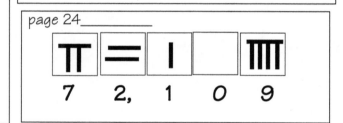

page 25_____

The mysterious dice puzzle

The answer is 32. The trick to doing this puzzle is to realize that all dice have a special property — the number of pips on opposite faces of a die always total 7. Since there are 5 dice, their hidden faces would equal 5x7=35 minus the 3 on the top die of the stack that you can see.

The knot puzzle

Cross your arms in front of you. While your arms are crossed, have each hand pick up an end of the rope. Holding the ends, uncross your arms. A knot is formed without either hand ever touching the end of the other hand's rope.

Penrose's balancing act

Put 2 Penroses on each side of the second weighing that has the 4 cubes on one side and the 2 pyramids and Penrose on the other.

The first weighing tells us whenever we have 2 cubes and a Penrose, we can replace them with 7 pyramids. So we can replace 4 cubes and 2 Penroses with 14 pyramids. So 14 pyramids balances 3 Penroses and 2 pyramids. Remove 2 pyramids from each side, and we have 12 pyramids balance 3 Penroses.

Therefore,

    4 pyramids balance 1 Penrose

page 29_____

1) 23 + x = 51. You can think about the equation, and reason x must be 28 because
23 + 28 = 51.

Or get x alone on one side of the equal sign by sub-tracting 23 from both sides of the equation.

$$23 + x = 51$$
$$\underline{-23 \qquad -23}$$
$$x = 29$$

2) $\dfrac{(2x)}{3}$ + 62= 74. To get x alone, first subtract 62 from both
$$\underline{-62 \quad -62}$$ sides of the equation.

$3 \times \left(\dfrac{2x}{3}\right)$ = 12 x 3 **Now** multiply both sides by 3.

So 2x = 36

You can get x alone by dividing both sides by 2. We get, x = 18.

page 34_____

Divide the picture into a grid as shown. Count the number of people in one little square of the grid. Multiply this by 25 because their are 25 little squares. Add to this the number of people there are on top who are outside the grid.
This a an estimate of the number of people.

page 34_____

(1) 23 – 7 = 16
(2) (5x2) + 6 =16
(3) (26-2) ÷ 6 =4
(4) $\sqrt{64}$ - 2 = 6
(5) (8-2)x(3-2) = 13-7

There may be more than one answer per problem.

page 39_____

The sewer puzzle
The circular lid is the only one that cannot fall through its hole no matter what angle you try. This is because on a circle all its points are equally distant from its center.

The number puzzle

$$
\begin{array}{ccccccl}
\boxed{1} & + & \boxed{9} & + & \boxed{7} & {\scriptstyle =14} & =17 \\
+ & & + & & + & & \\
\boxed{8} & + & \boxed{3} & + & \boxed{3} & & =14 \\
+ & & + & & + & & \\
\boxed{4} & + & \boxed{5} & + & \boxed{2} & & =11 \\
=13 & & =17 & & =12 & &
\end{array}
$$

Penrose's triangle puzzle
A triangle cannot be made with these three segments because the two shorter segments' lengths total 2 1/4 inches and the longest is 2 1/2 inches. So it is impossible for the two short segments to reach the ends of the longest segment.

solutions & answers section

page 42-43_____

The similar sets are:
set 3 and **set 6**.
The congruent sets are
set 1, set 4, set 5, and
set 7.
Notice **set 2** is neither
similar nor congruent.

_____
BIG CHALLENGE

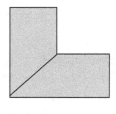

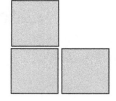

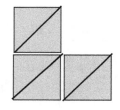

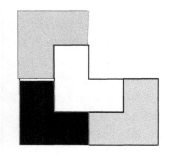

page 49_____

(a) The first move is to the diagonal corner. The next move is to move the dot to the next clockwise corner. Then repeat this pattern—move diagonally and then move clockwise one space.

(b) 10000 (to get the next term just add a 0 to the previous term, which is the same as multiplying it by 10)

(c) 5/18 (to get the next term, multiply the previous one by one-sixth)

(d) 61 (Two different processes are alternated for this sequence of numbers. To get the 2nd, 4th, 6th, ...terms, you double the previous term and add 1 to the result. For the 1st, 3rd, 5th, 7th,...terms, simply add 1 to its previous term.)

(e) These nine digits are arranged in alphabetical order. 8,5,4,9,1,7,6,3,2

eight, five, four, nine, one, seven, six, three, two

page 47_____

Here is Maya. Her outline appears when connecting the pairs of numbers in the order they were given. Just for fun, her graph was shaded on the inside.

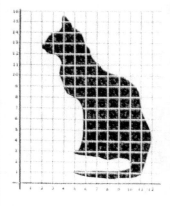

page 54_____

(1) The top of the circles appear to curve, but if a ruler is placed at their tops, all the circles lineup.

(2) The white rectangle appears larger than the black one, but they are are exactly the same size.

(3) The top side of the white trapezoid appears larger than the top side of the black one, but they are exactly the same size.

(4) The line on the left side of the rectangle appears to line up with the top line on the right side. But, it really lines up with the bottom line on the right side.

(5) The top and bottom curves of the ssssss seem the same size. But, when they are turned up-side down, we see they are not the same size.

solutions & answers section

page 57_____
Challenge 2
1+52=53
2+51=53
...
26+27=53
Since there are twenty-six 53s, the sum from 1 to 52 equals 26x53=**1,378**.

Now we find the sum of the counting number from 1 to 200.

1+200=201
2+199=201
...
100+101=201
The sum of these is one-hundred 201s=**20,100**, which is 100x201.

The difference of these two sum is the sum of the counting numbers from 52 to 200.
20,100-1,378=1**8,722**

Challenge 1
1+156=157
2+155=157
...
78+79=157

Since there are seventy-eight 157s, the sum is **12,246**, which is 78x157.

page 65_____

This picture is not a spiral but made up of concentric circles.

page 69_____

2) 1/6
3) 6 times
BIG CHALLENGE: 5/6

page 71_____

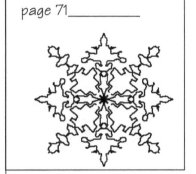

page 72____

The butterfly and the beetle each have one line of symmetry.

The circle of the half-orange has an infinite number of lines of symmetry. Each passes through the circle's center.

page 73_____

1. Capital letters with vertical symmetry are:
AHIMOTUVWXY
Capital letters with horizontal symmetry are:
BCDEHIKOX
Capital letters with both vertical and horizontal symmetry are: **HIOX**
Capital letters with no line symmetry are: **FGJLNPQRSZ**.
The message says: **CAN YOU READ THIS MESSAGE?**
2. (a) There are 5 lines of symmetry. Each lines passes through the flower's center and a tip of the five petals.

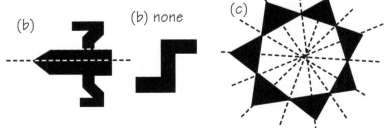

(b)　　　　(b) none　　　(c)

page 83_____

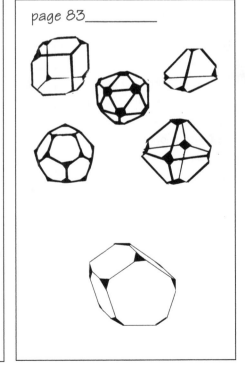

113

solutions & answers section

page 87_____

(a) 18
    + 48
    228

(b) Use the 5 rod and go down to row 8 and see the answer. Or, use the 8 rod and go down to row 5 and see the answer. **40**

(c) Line up rods 1,2, and 7. Go to row 9, and add these numbers as shown:
    9
    18
  + 63
    1143

(d) Think of 95x 64 as 95x60 plus 95x4
With the 9 & 5 rods together, first count down to row six and write:
    540
  + 300
5700
(The extra 0 making 54 into 540 and 30 into 300 is from the 60. If it were 600 two zeros would be used from the 600)

Now using the 9 and 5 rods count down to row 4, and we get:
    36
  + 20
  380

So 95x64=
5700 + 380=6080

NOTE: Any blank place on a rod can be thought of as a 0-place-holder. So going down to row 5 on rod 1 we see 5. This can be written as 5 or 05. They are the same value.

(e) Think of 123x57 as 123x50 plus 123x7.

Using the 1, 2, and 3 rods, and counting down to row 5 we get (remembering the extra zero from the 50):
    050
    100
  + 150
  6150

Using the rods 1, 2, and 3 again count down to row 7, and get:
    7
    14
  + 21
  861
The answer is 6150+861=**7011**

page 93 _____
<u>diameters</u> are: 2", 2.5" and 1".
<u>Circumferences around are</u>:
6 1/4"; 7 7/8"; and 3 1/8"

page 100 _____

a spiral · a chord · a radius

page 101 _____

THE COIN PUZZLE
The least number of weighings needed are 2. Here is how it can be done:
First weigh two piles of 3 coins each.
• If they balance each other, the counterfeit coin is one of the two coins not on the scale. Put them on the scale, and you will know the counterfeit coin.
• If the scale tipped with the 3 coins on each side, then the counterfeit coin is one of the 3 coins on the heavy side of the scale. Weigh two of these coins. If they balance, the counterfeit is the one not weighed. If they don't balance, the counterfeit coin is the heavier one.

continued on the next page

114

page 101 continued _____

MEASURING TIME PUZZLE
Turn them both over at the same time. The moment the 9 minute timer runs out, stop the 17 minute timer. The 17 minute timer now has 8 minutes remaining on it.
To measure 25 minutes, let the remaining 8 minutes of the 17 minute timer run and then just turn the 17 minute timer over again. You will have added 8 +17 and gotten 25 minutes.

THE FOUR 5S PUZZLE
(5+5)(5+5)=(10)(10)=100

THE TRIANGLE PUZZLES

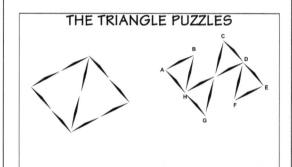

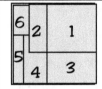

THE LAYING THE SQUARES PUZZLE

page 106 _____

(1) 32, 64, 128, 256, 512

(2) 512+256+128+64+32+16+8+4+2+1= 1,023

(a) 1 1 1 1 1 1 1 1 1 1

BIG CHALLENGE
5 is written as 101

16 is written as 10000

11 is written as 1011

page 108 _____
Here are some equations found in the 5x5 number square.
3+7=10
9+3=12
60÷4=15
20÷5=4
10-7=3
7x4=28
4x5=20
30÷6=5
60÷6=10
15÷3=5
3+12=15
4x15=60
There are many more. How many did you find?

page 108 _____
STAGE 1 One way to more the cards 3,2, & 1 to space C is:
1—>C, 2—>B, 1—>B, 3—>C, 1—>A, 2—>C, 1—>C

STAGE 2   1—>B, 2—>C, 1—>C, 3—>B, 1—>A, 2—>B, 1—>B, 4—>C, 1—>C, 2—>A,
1—>A, 3—>C, 1—>B, 2—>C, 1—>C,.

STAGE 3   1—>C, 2—>B, 1—>B, 3—>C, 1—>C, 2—>A, 1—>B, 2—>B, 1—>C, 4—>B,
1—>B, 2—>A, 1—>A, 3—>B, 1—>C, 2—>B, 1—>B, 5—>C, 1—>C, 2—>A, 1—>A, 3—>C,
1—>C, 2—>B, 1—>B, 3—>A, 1—>C, 2—>A, 1—>A, 4—>C, 1—>C, 2—>B, 1—>B, 3—>C,
1—>A, 2—>C, 1—>C

Penrose first decided to study mathematics when it was becoming increasingly impossible to get his mistress's attention. Whenever she would work on some project, he knew he would be neglected. He tried everything, from clawing furniture to pretending he was sleeping on her papers. Nothing seemed to work once she began reading her math books. Instead of moping around and feeling sorry for himself, he decided there must be something to this mathematics in which his mistress absorbed herself. He began to read the books she'd leave around. Penrose became fascinated with the ideas he read, and today he looks forward to math project time.

Mathematics teacher and consultant Theoni Pappas received her B.A. from the University of California at Berkeley in 1966 and her M.A. from Stanford University in 1967. Pappas is committed to demystifying mathematics and to helping eliminate the elitism and fear often associated with it. Among her recognitions, Pappas has received the *Excellence in Achievement Award* from the University of California Alumni Association, California Teachers Association *Merit Award for Innovative Teaching Developments,* the *Literacy Advocate Award* from the Public Enrichment Foundation, *Award of Merit* from Curriculum Products News, her book *Math For Kids & Other People Too!* was selected as an *Outstanding Title by the Parent Council® LTD..* Her books have been translated into Japanese, Finnish, Slovakian, Czech, Korean, Turkish, simplified and traditional Chinese, Portuguese, Italian, and Spanish.

Her innovative creations include *The Mathematics Calendar, The Children's Mathematics Calendar, The Mathematics Engagement Calendar, The Math-T-Shirt, and What Do You See?—an optical illusion slide show with text.* Pappas is also the author of the following books:

The Joy of Mathematics

More Joy of Mathematics

Math Talk

Fractals, Googols and Other Mathematical Tales

The Adventures of Penrose —The Mathematical Cat

The Further Adventures of Penrose

More Adventures from Penrose

Puzzles from Penrose

Math for Kids & Other People Too!

Math-A-Day Mathematical Footprints

Math Stuff

Do the math! The Magic of Mathematics

The Music of Reason

Mathematical Scandals

Greek Cooking for Everyone

Number & other math tales come alive

Her most recent book in her Penrose series is *More Adventures from of Penrose—The Mathematical Cat.*

Her latest book *Mathematical Journeys* was released in 2021.

Printed in the USA
CPSIA information can be obtained
at www.ICGtesting.com
JSHW060858021224
74593JS00004B/3

9 781884 550324